Arizona Homecoming

Pamela Tracy

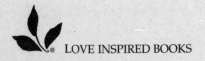

LOVE INSPIRED BOOKS

Recycling programs
for this product may
not exist in your area.

ISBN-13: 978-0-373-81922-5

Arizona Homecoming

www.Harlequin.com

Printed in U.S.A.

"Let no debt remain outstanding,
except the continuing debt to love one another, for
he who loves his fellowman has fulfilled the law."
—*Romans* 13:8

To every parent who looks out the door waiting for a child—be he ten, twenty, thirty or older—to waltz up the path and be welcomed.

Chapter One

Yellowish-brown shards rose to the surface at the edge of Donovan Russell's shovel. They were a startling contrast to the hard mud-brown dirt he'd been digging in.

"Should have left well enough alone," he muttered.

After a few run-ins with local special interests—okay, one rabble-rouser with amazing dark brown eyes, on a mission—the Baer custom-built house was finally back on schedule but a bit over budget. Not that money mattered. Just last night George Baer had called asking for a circular driveway along with one that led to the backyard and a three-car garage. As the site architect and builder, Donovan had merely said, *Yes, sir, we can do that.*

Looking at the marking paint that now highlighted where the circular drive might go, Dono-van decided maybe he shouldn't have gotten so annoyed at the one spot where the dirt curved upward and kept his imagined drive from being level.

Annoyed was one thing; acting on it another. A backhoe would have been easier to use on this alkaline clay-based dirt that threatened to bend his shovel. Yes, it was that hard.

"I overreacted," Donovan muttered. Not that there was anyone to hear him. He was miles from the nearest neighbor and living alone in a camper.

Adding a circular driveway would not take that much time, and if he needed to start his next custom job a few weeks late, no one would protest. In his line of work, behind schedule was a way of life. One he personally didn't appreciate.

Donovan hated when his schedule changed. Still, the change was on Baer's dime, and Donovan's goal was to please the customer. Someday, he wanted to please himself, build homes, tree houses, businesses that matched their environment, were one of a kind and affordable.

He had two years left with Tate Luxury Homes. He'd promised to finish his contract and pay off his debt to Nolan Tate, and he'd keep his word. Breaking up with Olivia Tate had been a serious step backward in recovering from a poor career choice. The breakup had, however, been a huge step forward in finding peace.

Not that he'd experienced much peace lately.

His next job was in Palmdale, California. The

sun was more polite there. After that, three jobs in Florida. Then, the freedom to choose where, when and how often he worked.

He dug the shovel in a bit deeper, ignoring the sweat gathering at his hairline.

A Nebraska boy through and through, Donovan couldn't believe that at five in the morning *in June* the Arizona sun was able to stretch out her fingers with an extremely heated "I'm here for the rest of the day" massage.

Fine, tomorrow he'd start work at four.

Who would choose to live in this heat? Almost immediately, he smiled. His favorite special-interest advocate was a slip of a woman named Emily Hubrecht. She'd shown up at the job site the first day, spouting something about the property next to the Baers', empty and neglected, that had yielded some Native American pottery a few decades ago. She was sure more was to be found, maybe even a burial ground, and that the home he was building might prevent a historic discovery of epic proportions.

Her words, not his.

He had, however, enjoyed the few weeks she'd poked and prodded the land. Emily was more entertaining than the men working with him. She'd found no proof, and so his permits had been given.

She hadn't changed her way of thinking.

It was something they had in common. They

could see potential even in the dirt on a forlorn piece of the Arizona desert.

When she'd scowled at the permits in his hand and raised defiant eyes to his, he found himself promising, *I find any arrowheads, pots, or bows and arrows, I'll give them right to you.* He'd do it, too, because it was the right thing to do.

The dirt gave way to something with more substance as Donovan gently nudged with his shovel.

Bones.

A brief sorrow washed over him at the thought of some long-ago child standing over an aged Fido and saying goodbye. Maybe it was time to get a four-legged companion. Not that Donovan was ever lonely. He was far too busy for that.

At least that's what he told himself late at night in a tiny camper with one bed, one table, a minuscule kitchen and a bathroom so small that taking a shower meant one foot in and one foot out of the tub.

Except for the heat, Donovan enjoyed his time here. This part of Arizona was rich in history and the kind of rural lifestyle he'd grown up with. Everyone knew each other. He'd not been in town more than two days before the waitress at the Miner's Lamp knew his favorite meal and the grocery store manager knew what brand of cereal he preferred. Even the Hubrecht family, save Emily, seemed to like him. Her father had built the Lost

Dutchman Ranch's main building and kept asking Donovan for advice on updating.

Then, too, Donovan had received a dozen invitations to church, even from the enchanting Emily, and one marriage proposal. He'd nicely refused them all.

Moving the shovel, he unearthed another bone. The Baer home stood a good twenty miles from its nearest neighbor. Strange place for a dog to be buried. A homeless mutt might have died on the spot, but this was somewhat deep and definitely had been here awhile.

Smokey Begay, the construction crew's foreman, parked on what would someday be a real driveway. Stepping from his truck, he squinted, and then came to stand beside Donovan. "What are you doing?"

Eerie how the man knew every time Donovan needed something, whether it be advice, a tool or simply another hand to get a job done quicker.

"Baer wants a circular driveway, too," Donovan explained. "I thought I'd dig a rough outline."

"Why did you stop digging?"

"Bones," Donovan said, only this time he wasn't thinking of a crying boy and a beloved dog.

Smokey took a step backward, his demeanor going from curious to stoic in a blink. "This is not good."

"I tend to agree." Over the years Donovan had found old toys, bullets and once a vintage pair of glasses—very Benjamin Franklinish. He kept those on the dashboard of his truck.

Donovan pushed his shovel deeper in the hard dirt, his gut already telling him what he didn't want to know. "Dogs do have femurs?" he asked Smokey hopefully, his question more a statement.

"Yes, but not even a Great Dane would have a femur like that," Smokey said.

It took only five minutes to uncover the human skull.

Emily Hubrecht finished pinning the flyer advertising Apache Creek Library Celebrates Sixty Years to the bulletin. Then, she put up a separate flyer about the hour of Native American storytelling she'd be donating to the library to help with the festivities.

It had been a while since she'd made time to do what she loved most: storytelling. During the school year she visited the sixth grade for American History Month. Every once in a while, she'd get a call from Phoenix or Tucson asking for her services. In reality, most of her storytelling happened as she guided the museum's visitors up and down the aisles. That didn't feel like storytelling, though. It felt more like a documentary narrative.

Outside, gravel crunched, heralding visitors. Emily watched as two people exited the minivan that had parked in front of her museum. She waited for a dozen kids to burst from the doors but not even one pigtailed head showed.

So far today, twelve patrons had signed the museum's register. Emily wanted, prayed for, a hundred and fifty. How could people not fall in love the with Apache Creek's artifacts, history and folklore?

She blamed the museum's name. The Lost Dutchman Museum. Really? Only a small portion of the museum dealt with old Jacob Waltz—nicknamed the Lost Dutchman—and his irrelevant, misguided contribution to the history of the Superstition Mountains. The majority of displays had to do with the ancient and not-so-ancient inhabitants who'd left behind tangible relics and folklore.

The woman from the van was dressed to the nines and didn't look the type to be impressed with old mining paraphernalia or Native American treasures. She seemed more suited to a Porsche than minivan. Emily moved closer to the window. Ah, a rental.

The man appeared much older, wearing white pants and a suit jacket. Those pants would stay clean sixty seconds in this museum immersed in history and dust.

They entered the foyer with a sense of entitlement. Emily didn't mind. These were the kind of tourists who might spend money on one of the many books in the tiny gift area, maybe even buy a Native American woven blanket. "May I help you?"

"We're looking for pieces from old movie sets?" the man answered. "To buy. We heard John Wayne liked this part of Arizona, and I'm a collector."

"We did have many Westerns shot here," Emily began. "Not just John Wayne, but Audie—"

"Just John Wayne," the man said firmly.

Emily shook her head. "I've a few things from the days when Westerns were shot here but they're not on display yet and none are for sale."

The couple turned away without even glancing past the foyer, heading for the exit.

Emily tried again. "We've got Native American artifacts thousands of years old and—"

They closed the front door behind them before Emily could try enticing them with her storytelling skills that would transport them to another era.

"John Wayne would appreciate my artifacts and stories," Emily muttered and glanced at the clock. It was almost noon. She closed at four, when the sun shot past high and went to *burning*. Most tourists would be thinking of eating and returning to their hotels for a dip in the pool.

She headed back to the Salado room. It was tiny compared to the rest, with just a few bowls and farming utensils on display. After unlocking the glass cabinet, she pulled a pair of gloves from her back pocket, put them on and then retrieved a tiny reddish bowl with faded black-and-white paint etched on the sides. As she walked back to her office, her fingers gently gripped the bowl, reveling in an artifact from such a distant era.

Who had it belonged to? A young bride, a grandmother, a wife in charge of feeding many? Emily was half–Native American, from the Hopi tribe, and was writing her family's history. One of her many projects. Her father said she'd get more done if she could settle on doing one job at a time.

She didn't like the word *time*. Time was something you could run out of, like her mother had. Emily didn't want someone a thousand years from today to say, *Yes, I've heard of the Hopi, but really, all they left were a few belongings we can fit in this tiny corner of the room.* Emily wanted the world to know about her mom's family from the Kykotsmovi Village, near Holbrook. She wanted to paint with words the Soyal ceremony when young girls received their kachinas. She wanted the Hopi Butterfly Dance to live on through storytelling as well as practice.

When she made it back to her desk, she took out a box and started fitting packing paper inside. She was lending the bowl to the Heard Museum in Phoenix. They were doing a display of forgotten tribes and had contacted her just two weeks ago, wanting to find out what she knew.

They read her paper on the Salado. Her first published piece as a college student majoring in Native American studies. The curator hadn't even known she was a local, hadn't known she was the new curator of the Lost Dutchman Museum.

A tumbleweed scooted across the parking lot and disappeared down the same road as the minivan.

Emily secured the bowl, sure that it wouldn't suffer a crack even if the Phoenix Suns used the package for basketball practice, and after taking off her gloves, headed for the tiny break room, thinking she'd eat lunch although she wasn't hungry.

The phone rang before she managed three steps.

"Emily," Sam Miller said. He was part of the four-man police team that kept Apache Creek safe.

"What is it, Sam?"

"They've uncovered bones at the end of Ancient Trails Road, the Baer place."

An epic house in the middle of nowhere. There'd been protests, mostly from Emily, who filed petitions about protecting the wilderness and the land that was once home to the Native people. She'd managed to delay a permit until she had a chance to look over the property. She just knew it had been a Native American village centuries ago. All her research pointed to that spot. The architect, one Donovan Russell, had taken to saluting her should she come close, as if she were some... well, never mind that. And, at least saluting was preferable to the irritated look he'd given her the last time she'd filed a protest.

"How old?"

"Old enough. It's a skeleton, and it's been there awhile and could be a Native American." He didn't sound happy.

She'd been right all along.

The Baers were building right where an ancient settlement had thrived. There had to be a plethora of artifacts just waiting to be found.

What if today was the day?

Emily didn't smile. Chances were the location had already been compromised. Now, Donovan Russell would have to listen. If he'd damaged the skeleton or anything surrounding it, he'd have desecrated a venerable object.

A felony!

He should have listened to her.

Chapter Two

Emily stepped from her truck, giving a quick appraisal of the area—brown dirt, cacti and the distant Superstition Mountains—before heading for Officer Sam Miller and royal-pain Donovan Russell.

Sam she'd known forever. He was still the too-tall, never-quite-fitting-his-frame boy, now a man. When he was hanging around her oldest sister, Emily figured he'd turn into a professional skateboarder or something like that. Instead, he'd gone away to college and come back with a degree in criminal justice and hired on as a cop.

"Care to help?" she said to him.

Sam half smiled. He wasn't overly fond of dead bodies and happily turned them over to her or immigration—usually immigration because this area had more than its share of illegal immigrants hurrying through and falling victim to the weather or bad circumstances. He was much more comfortable dealing with the mundane.

He'd already cordoned off the area around the skeleton. Both he and Donovan stood by the edge of the tape, talking. Judging by the looks on their faces, they'd been discussing her.

"When did you find the remains?" she asked.

"About five thirty this morning," Donovan answered. She wouldn't exactly call him welcoming.

"I was roughing out a circular drive," he continued. "There was an upheaval in the dirt bothering me so I decided to smooth it out. Took me over twenty minutes to get about four inches dug. That's when I started unearthing bone shards. Next thing I knew, I had a skull."

"You touch anything?"

"Just the shovel. Once I'd uncovered enough to realize what I had, I called the police."

Sam Miller added, "Jamal Begay was here."

It took Emily a few seconds before she responded, "Jamal was here?"

"He got here a few moments before I found the skull," Donovan stated.

"Bad timing." Emily knew Smokey. He was a good man, with a family, and superstitious as all get-out.

Both Sam and Donovan nodded.

It was a very clean site. The dirt was packed hard, no footprints. Then, too, this skeleton had been around awhile, so even if there were any disturbances in the area, chances were they'd be recent. She took out gloves and removed two baggies from her jean pockets. Sam came to stand beside her. "What do you want me to do?"

"Nothing at the moment."

"Aren't you going to wait for the medical examiner?" Donovan asked.

"Why?" Emily looked up at him. He couldn't be more different than Sam. He was taller than she was, but then, who wasn't? She put him at five-ten, all muscle and what her father would call a scrapper. His honey-brown hair was cut short, and he had an impish smile.

Usually. He looked a little pale right now. Finding human bones tended to have that effect.

"You think I can't handle this?" She rather liked the displaced look on his face.

"I told you Emily is who we call," Sam said.

"In case the remains prove to be Native American," Donovan agreed. "Tell me they're not."

She stepped over the cordon tape and bent down next to the remains. "Too soon to tell."

"But don't we need a medical examiner to—"

Sam interrupted, "We're too small to have our own medical examiner. If this turns out to be a crime scene or not a Native jurisdiction," he nodded toward Emily, "we'll call the Maricopa County medical examiner's office."

"What have you done so far?" Emily asked Sam.

"Photos and call you."

"What's next?" Donovan's voice implied he didn't want to know.

"Finish digging up the body, take more photos, probably call in an entomologist, sieve the grave, search a grid for belongings."

"Entomologist?" Donovan queried.

"I'm not skilled enough nor do I have the tools to determine the true postmortem interval. We'll want to know the time of death."

"How long will that take?"

Emily smiled. "Oh, you're going to be stuck with me for a long time."

Gloating, that's what Emily Hubrecht was doing. Turning to Sam, Donovan again asked, "You sure she's the one you had to call?"

Sam nodded as they watched Emily head back to a Lost Dutchman Ranch truck that rivaled Donovan's in size. One foot on the back bumper, she hopped twice on the other foot in order to swing her body over the tailgate. Emily might claim to be five foot four, but Donovan knew better. He'd put in enough cabinets to gauge who could reach the top shelf and who couldn't. Emily was a footstool short, making her a hair over five foot three.

She opened the tool chest that stretched across the bed of her truck, pulled out a large black canvas bag and tossed it to the ground before jumping down to retrieve it. She handled it with ease and was already standing beside the skull before Donovan thought to offer to carry it for her.

"She worked up in South Dakota restoring an Indian burial ground that grave robbers had desecrated," Sam said. "She has a degree in cultural anthropology and knows more about bones than anyone else in town."

"How do you know all that?"

"Small town?

"And why—"

Sam interrupted, "It also makes her qualified to help work a crime scene. If we have one."

"Might not be a crime scene," Emily said. "Could be somebody who just lay down and died of old age."

Donovan looked at the area that had already been cordoned off. "Why here? It's the middle of nowhere."

She gave him a look only a female knew how to form. "This wasn't always the middle of nowhere."

Of course she'd bring up her supposed village and how the home he was building encroached upon the remnants. Those had been her words.

"She's especially good with old bones," Sam said. "The department keeps her on retainer."

Oh, how Donovan wished he'd found a dog.

They watched her for a moment as she took photos and drew a few pictures in a small notebook. There was something intimate, respectful in her movements. But just the thought of working so closely with a skull, let alone the makings of a whole skeleton, gave Donovan the heebie-jeebies.

He cleared his throat—no way did he want Sam to think him a wimp—and quietly asked, "So, Navajos avoid the dead?" He wasn't really thinking about Smokey; he was thinking about Emily. She was Native American but must not be Navajo because she wasn't leaving. It didn't surprise him that she was the one who Sam had called.

"Something about the good leaving with the soul and the evil remaining with the body."

She spoke matter-of-factly, clearly honoring what Smokey and a few of the other construction workers believed. He wondered if it was what she believed, and if so, why she'd chosen such a career path.

Come to think of it, he wasn't quite certain what her career path was. At first, when she'd been all over him with petitions and threats of cease and desist, he'd thought she was some sort of activist. But, when she had finally handed him a business card, it stated that she was a "storyteller." Whatever that was. Then, he'd found out she was also the curator at the Lost Dutchman Museum. Two weeks ago he'd gone to the Lost Dutchman Ranch for dinner, and she was waiting tables. If not for her, he'd have made it his favorite stop. The locale was perfect, the food great, and he liked Jacob, the owner and Emily's father. But, quite frankly, he didn't trust her not to put *really* hot sauce in his food.

"Who are you today?" he asked.

She blinked up at him. "What do you mean?"

"Curator? Waitress? Storyteller? Pseudo medical examiner?"

"Civilian forensic consultant to the Apache Creek PD."

He almost chuckled, almost asked her if she was old enough. Wisely, he didn't. He was already on her bad side, and annoying her wouldn't get him back to work any quicker.

Donovan knew exactly what Emily hoped to find. He just couldn't remember the name of the tribe she was so enamored with. He thought a moment. It wasn't one of the common tribes. He'd never heard it until she'd started poking around, getting in his way, insisting that Baer was building on a historic gold mine.

At least that's how she'd put it after she accused him of encroaching on her remnants.

Sam's phone sounded, and Donovan heard just enough to know that the police officer had obtained some sort of search warrant for excavating the body.

This was going to turn into a major hassle, Donovan just knew it. He headed back to his company truck and snagged a bottled water from his cooler before leaning against the door to study Emily. To think, just an hour ago he'd been happy because everything was on schedule. Now, he was down to a... Donovan tried to stop thinking the term *skeleton crew*.

He couldn't.

Smokey, acting as if he was late for an important meeting, had left the premises not two minutes after the bones surfaced. He'd called his two cousins, coworkers, and they weren't coming back any time soon. Only one of Donovan's team showed up. John Westerfield had arrived ten minutes before Emily. He'd spent most of the time sitting in his truck, talking on the phone and no doubt trying to convince his wife that it wasn't his fault he wouldn't be working today. This wasn't the type of job that paid if hours weren't put in. He'd not been a happy man when he drove away.

Donovan would have to ask Emily how to get his crew back and working.

"So," Sam Miller said, hanging up his phone and going to one knee by Emily, careful not to disturb anything, "you find any personal effects yet?"

"Not yet, but I've just begun."

"You find bodies often?" Donovan asked. George Baer had extolled the lack of crime in Apache Creek. It was one of the reasons he and his wife were retiring here.

"Enough," Sam said. "We're what you'd call a high-intensity drug trafficking area."

"Marijuana?"

Sam shrugged. "Along with whatever else will sell."

"So," Donovan said, "I might not be looking at a burial ground but instead a drug deal gone wrong?"

"Could be. I've never discovered a burial ground. I've also never discovered a whole skeleton. When I find drug deals gone wrong, they're usually a bit more ripe."

Emily made a face. Donovan looked over at his camper. All one would need was a pair of scissors to break in. Not something he wanted to think about. He decided to change the topic somewhat. "Would Smokey be just as put off by Anglo remains as Native American?"

"Pretty sure," Emily said. "Good and evil don't care the race."

Donovan nodded, took out his cell phone and walked toward the home. The sun followed him, burning his arms and reminding him that it was high noon and well past break time. He'd been doing nothing but standing around the past hour or so. No reason to be tired.

Stepping inside he took in the fresh-paint smell, the hint of wood and the white dust particles that were everywhere. Sometimes when he got off work and showered in his camper, the top of his head looked like the before commercial for a dandruff shampoo.

Yesterday he'd been inside the house working on baseboards with a portable evacuative cooler blowing on him. His crew, all locals, had been painting and making fun of him. Didn't bother him. They didn't turn red three minutes after working in the sun. Three of his crew were Navajo and then he had John. They were all good workers, talented and easy to get along with. They all thought the house going up at 2121 Ancient Trails Road a bit extravagant for the parts, but didn't care. They were working.

Exactly what Donovan wanted to be doing at this moment. Usually, when it got to this stage in the process, he relaxed.

But, he realized, he'd not relaxed at all during his time in Apache Creek. It had been one thing after another. Thanks mostly to Emily Hubrecht.

Quickly, he called George Baer and told the man about the skeleton. George's only questions were "Can they halt progress?" followed by "Can they reclaim the land?"

"I'm pretty sure they can halt progress, temporarily. You'll need to contact a lawyer for more information. The officer in charge of the case doesn't think they can reclaim the land. You might, however, be responsible for the cost of moving the body and anything else discovered."

Silence. Anyone else, and Donovan would assume they were assessing cost. Not George Baer. He'd be thinking about time and possibly media exposure. The man liked his privacy. Thus the end-of-the-road residence in out-of-the-way Apache Creek, Arizona. It was a custom-build situation unlike any Donovan had ever worked on before.

After Baer told him to do what he had to do, Donovan disconnected the call and stayed in the kitchen, looking out the window at the talented Miss Hubrecht. Even on her knees digging up bones, she managed to look beautiful. Long black hair was caught back in a ponytail that swayed while she used both a brush and a small shovel-like tool to free the skeleton without damaging it.

Nothing about this build was ordinary.

He'd been working for Tate Luxury Homes for the past three years, mostly because he'd fallen in love with Olivia Tate. After a while, he'd realized she was a bit like the luxury home he was building for George Baer: all show and no heart.

Donovan hoped that Olivia found the right man for her. He wasn't that man. Before he'd even started dating Olivia, Donovan had borrowed money from Nolan Tate, her father, and now it would take at least five homes and two years to repay the debt. What was best about the current location was, while uncomfortable, it was far away from Olivia and her tantrums.

Maybe *uncomfortable* was too kind a word. George Baer's house, so far, had no electricity, no plumbing and no urban comfort.

Emily looked up, caught him watching her and looked away. He felt a moment's disappointment. Why? He'd be out of Apache Creek in a little over a month.

But, unable to resist, he glanced back at her, mesmerized by the fire in her eyes and thinking that such a look shouldn't be there because of a skeleton.

Her hands kept moving, gently uncovering what Donovan wished had stayed buried. Then, when he could see she had dug well past the ribs, she stilled.

He took one step in her direction, half pulled by curiosity and half pulled by the instinct to be there if she needed him.

Sam got there first. "What did you find?"

"My guess, based on his teeth and the condition of the bones, is we have a male skeleton between twenty-five and forty years old. I can only estimate how long he's been buried here. I believe, though, an entomologist would agree with my findings. If I were going through missing-person reports, I'd focus on at least the last fifty years."

Donovan let out the breath he hadn't known he was holding. Not an ancient burial ground.

"You'll want to call Maricopa and the medical examiner, though," Emily said. "There's a knife next to the body."

Donovan breathed in. His custom-built home had just gone from burial ground to crime scene.

At least if it had been a burial ground, Emily Hubrecht would have provided a diversion.

Chapter Three

"Find anything?" Jane de la Rosa asked when Emily walked through the museum's front door.

Emily couldn't remember Jane or Jane's mother not being a part of her life. Jane's mother, Patti, used to work at the front desk of the Lost Dutchman Ranch. She'd been let go a few years ago. Jacob, Emily's father, said it was because his girls were doing more. Emily knew it had more to do with Patti's attempts to become more to him than just an employee.

Jane often filled in at the museum when Emily needed someone to spell her. What Jane didn't know about history, she made up for with enthusiasm.

Hesitating and maybe just now letting it all sink in, Emily slowly said, "Yes."

"Because you look like you dug all the way to Tucson."

Since no cars were in the parking lot, meaning no visitors, Emily felt free to share, ending with "The skeleton was no more than two feet down right in the middle of nowhere. Not even close to the old trail leading to the Superstition Mountains."

"Poor man." Jane immediately bowed her head, engaging in a silent prayer. Emily followed her example, reminding herself that what she'd found today had been someone's son, possibly husband, maybe father, maybe friend, and deserved respect.

"Find anything else?" Jane asked.

The skeleton had waited decades to be discovered. The Maricopa County medical examiner would no doubt make him wait a few more days. After all, the skeleton wasn't going anywhere. Sam Miller hadn't even bothered telling Emily not to talk about the discovery. Already, four construction workers knew and probably four wives and maybe even a child or two. In Apache Creek, when a girl sneezed, the *bless you* might come from three miles away. That's how fast news traveled.

"I stopped digging when I got to the pelvis, which let me know I had a male. There was a knife right next to the hip bone."

"Recognize it?" Jane's eye lit up.

"Of course not. I left it half-buried. No way do I want to compromise a crime scene. All I'd need to do is anger the wrong official and suddenly my position identifying local Native American sites would be in jeopardy. I told Donovan Russell not to build there."

It was true, too. Quite a few people wanted the past to be the past and let progress reign. Case in point, Donovan Russell and the absent George Baer, who'd employed him. Lately, it felt as if she and the townspeople of Apache Creek were in opposition with the mayor and a few other major players, like business owners and Realtors. Their little town was in danger of losing what Emily considered its heart. Others might call it quaintness. Not Emily. Apache Creek's history set it apart from every other small town. How could people not appreciate it?

"Those acres of land have been for sale since before you were born," Jane said. "You can't be mad because someone finally purchased them and is now building. You've given Donovan enough grief."

"You're sticking up for him because he's a good tipper."

"And careful with his money, an overall nice guy. Besides, I've known you since you were in diapers. You get your teeth in something and you don't know when to let go."

"I'm right more than I'm wrong. And—" Emily wagged her finger "—when I was in diapers you were just eight years old and thought Batman was real."

"He is real," Jane teased before sobering. "You've

got to accept that change happens, and for a reason. I can understand you wanting to preserve a two-hundred-year-old Native American village, but I don't see a village there. Sometimes you go too far."

Emily knew where this was going.

"You," Jane continued, "need to forgive Randall Tucker for tearing down the Majestic Hotel. It stood empty for more than twenty years."

Now greeting visitors who turned off the highway was an apartment complex that looked like a million others. Boring. And she'd purchased the remnants of the Majestic's history on her own dime or they'd have been lost. It was history. Apache Creek used to be a favorite shooting location for Hollywood Westerns, and the Majestic had been the hotel the actors, directors and such had stayed at. She had old movie posters, props and even an old script from a Roy Rogers flick.

It wasn't that she loved Roy Rogers—she didn't remember him. Or that she loved old Westerns. She didn't. But, when looking at history, the way the movies depicted culture and mind-set was priceless, a teaching opportunity.

The couple that had been here this morning hadn't had a clue. They loved the persona of John Wayne, not the real man or the real history.

Looking in her mirror, she had to laugh. She could be right out of an old Western herself, with a dark smudge across her nose, sunburned cheeks and mussed hair. Jane hadn't been far off when she'd questioned how much dirt Emily brought back with her. She just wished her time spent had done something to halt Donovan's progress.

One custom-built home, with a backdrop of the Superstition Mountains, would surely lead to another until soon there'd be a gated community—pimples marring the mountains' beauty.

Jane already had her purse on her shoulder when Emily returned to the front. "Two families stopped by. They loved the place."

Yeah, Emily loved it, too, but she needed a thousand more people to show a little love if the museum was going to survive.

Donovan looked at the calendar: Friday. Exactly one week since he'd uncovered the bones. He hated being behind schedule. Once Emily had determined the remains were fairly recent and a crime scene, she'd filled out a report, turning it over to the medical examiners.

What a show that was. The medical examiner and his crew had arrived this past Tuesday—guess Monday was a busy day—with what looked like tool chests. The remains were carried away in individual labeled bags on Thursday.

"What now, boss?" John Westerfield asked, bringing Donovan's attention back to the present.

"Not a circular drive, that's for sure." Donovan glanced at the cordon tape still waving in the tepid Arizona wind. In the past week, what they'd accomplished was piecemeal at most. He'd found it distracting to deal with the various law-enforcement personnel as well as reporters looking for clues that clearly weren't there.

Except for the knife.

Since the discovery, he and John had done indoor work with lots of interruptions that had Donovan—who'd been instructed by Baer to cooperate fully but not to mention his name—saying, "the homeowner" this and "the homeowner" that…

Smokey and his cousins had taken the whole week off and Donovan could only hope they'd show up on Monday. When, according to Sam Miller, they could resume work with no one interrupting them.

Donovan was disturbed by quite a few things, and they weren't all work related.

At five, he called it a day. John picked up his lunch box and drove off.

Donovan had other plans. He headed to the camper behind Baer's not-quite-finished home and quickly showered and changed clothes before heading for the Lost Dutchman Ranch. Exactly one week after Emily predicted, *You're going to be stuck with me for a long time*, he pulled into a parking spot in front of a huge barn and walked the path to her family's restaurant.

He hadn't been stuck with her. No, he'd been stuck with a dark-haired, fortysomething male medical examiner with two trainees, who showed up in a white van, carrying rakes, sifters, trowels and brushes. They weren't afraid to get dirty, but Donovan got the idea that his crime scene had taken a whole day longer than necessary because the ME was using it as his trainees' hands-on classroom.

The only thing Donovan had overheard was the ME showing his students evidence of severe arthritis in the bones.

Donovan wasn't really in the mood to eat at the Lost Dutchman Ranch's restaurant. It would have been easier to eat on Main Street at the Miner's Lamp. No, not true. Every diner would be looking at him. A good number of locals would have headed over, hands out for a shake or slap on the back, and started a conversation with, "So tell me about…"

At least here, at the Lost Dutchman Ranch, most of the patrons were from out of town, if not out of state. Maybe they'd not heard yet.

Truth was, he'd been summoned. Jacob Hubrecht wanted to hire him for some odd building job, and Donovan was intrigued.

Stepping from his truck, he took a deep breath, smelling mulch, plant life, animals and most of all barbecue. It was ten times better than the dust, particle board, glue and paint he smelled at work.

When he grew close to finishing the Baer place, the landscapers would swoop in. He couldn't help but think George Baer had made a mistake. The man wanted artificial grass and even a putting green. To Donovan's way of thinking, Jacob Hubrecht's ranch was the real beauty. The house was original—Donovan's favorite kind of building—and complemented its surrounding. Emily had grown up in a breathtaking place with vibrant colors and personality.

His parents' place had been about this size, too, but they'd used the land for cattle, not horses and vacationers. Thus, no pool, no pretend schoolhouse and no covered-wagon decor. It had been an all-work-and-no-play kind of place, especially for Donovan, an only child.

Nebraska didn't have anything that equaled the Superstition Mountains. But suddenly he missed the Mytal sunset and the taste of his mother's mashed potatoes and his father's baritone voice singing a gospel song.

There were no skeletons buried in their yard. That was for sure. Just a deep love and appreciation for the family, for the land and for the Lord. Donovan rarely went home and struggled with a sense that he'd failed when it came to the commandment "Honor your father and your mother so that you may live long in the land your God has given you."

Probably why Donovan had stopped attending church: guilt.

His dad would say the land was the Russell

Dairy Farm. Unfortunately, his choice *not* to take over the family business had festered into a permanent wound that neither father nor son could heal.

Donovan walked toward the dining room, thinking that big-city people didn't know what they were missing. This was a happening place, a joyful place, with family portraits and wall decorations that were Native American heirlooms or present-day rodeo memorabilia instead of plastic or mass-produced knickknacks. He spotted Jacob sitting with Emily and another dark-haired woman, and headed for the rancher's table, arriving before he was spotted and just as Jacob Hubrecht was saying, "That would be like putting a Band-Aid on a broken dam. You can't stop Donovan from building any more than you can stop progress. Apache Creek is going to grow." He looked out one of the windows and nodded toward the panoramic view of the Superstition Mountains. "You can blame them."

To Donovan's surprise, Jacob—without taking his eyes off the mountains—added, "Right, Donovan?"

Not exactly the way Donovan wanted the evening to begin. "That's correct, sir."

Jacob grinned as he looked at Emily, who made a face as if she'd just swallowed a pickle. She had the same glimmer of passion in her eyes that she'd had last week while examining the skeleton, and there was a little smudge of brown under the left side of her chin, letting him know she'd been playing in the dirt again.

Instead of asking her whose dirt she was digging in today, he said, "I didn't come here to change Apache Creek. It's perfect the way it is. I'm building one home. I'm a builder, not a developer. And I'm not the home owner."

"If you want to stop more homes from going up, you'll need to buy the land yourself." This advice was aimed at Emily and came from a tall blonde woman.

Emily frowned, and Jacob stepped in. "Donovan, you've not met all my girls. It's a rare occurrence they're all here. Eva's my oldest and will take your order. I hope you've not eaten."

Now Donovan saw the resemblance. Eva looked a lot like Jacob, light haired, while Emily and the other sister must take after a dark-haired mother. And Eva was obviously pregnant. Her advice about buying the land was sound, and Donovan wondered if Jacob could afford to do so.

"I'll take iced tea and help myself to your pulled-pork sandwich with homemade chips." It was what he'd had last time he ate here. The aroma had lured him the moment he stepped out of his truck.

"No one can afford to buy all the land that needs to be preserved in this area," Emily protested, "and no one should have to. It should be made into a state park, part of the Superstition land trust."

"We didn't find Native American remains," Donovan said, claiming the only vacant chair, which happened to be next to Emily.

"You could have. He wasn't buried very deep. Decades of wind could have covered him up. And just because he's not more than a century old doesn't mean he's not Native American, and—"

"Emily," the sister at the table said gently.

While Emily continued talking, ignoring her big sister, Donovan studied the other female, a taller, more slender version of Emily. When Emily finally stopped her impassioned tirade with a har-rumph, the woman held out her hand and said, "Since no one is going to introduce me, I'll do it myself. I'm Elise."

"Donovan Russell. I met your fiancé Cooper a few days ago. I stopped by his outfitters store. He told me all about gold panning."

She looked at her little sister with an indulgent expression, and then back at Donovan. "And my little sister has told me all about you."

"All good?" he joked.

"I like to judge for myself. I've been keeping up with what the house you're building looked like. So far, I'm not sure."

Donovan doubted she'd be impressed, considering where Elise lived. The Lost Dutchman Ranch blended in with its surroundings, making a visitor take in the whole package: house, land, mountains. George Baer definitely wanted visitors to notice only his house.

No, not the house, but his money.

"Then, I went to your website," Elise continued. "You've done some impressive homes."

"Back in Omaha? Or the last three years?" he asked.

"Definitely back in the Omaha area."

Made sense. There he'd not been building true luxury homes. He thought back to the first house he'd worked on with Tate Luxury Homes in Springfield, Illinois. It had been a fourteen-thousand-square-foot split-level mansion with marble floors and two elevators. The master bedroom had a fireplace and a waterfall! Two of the bedrooms were for little girls and had castles with stairs and a tower, jutting from one wall.

For show.

There'd also been a two-tiered Jacuzzi with a flat-screen television and its own bar.

"And you build tree houses." A young boy spoke right in Donovan's ear before pulling a chair over to sit next to him. Excitement emphasized each word.

"My nephew, Timmy. Eva's stepson," Emily introduced.

Here was the type of future homeowner Donovan wanted to build for. The boy promptly set some Legos on the table and started creating as he spoke. "Emily found some pictures of your tree houses. Grandpa saw them, too, and he wants you to build us Tinytown."

Tinytown?

Emily had looked at his personal website?

"Timmy, I hadn't had a chance to get around to discussing business with Mr. Russell," Jacob chided without sounding the least bit perturbed.

"You searched for me on the internet?" Donovan asked Emily.

"Elise did," Emily said. "But my motto's always been Know Your Friends but Know Your Enemies More."

"What?" Donovan couldn't help but laugh. He had a few proverbs he'd like to spout, too.

Emily didn't seem to appreciate his mirth.

"I'm not your enemy. I'm a custom-home builder hired to do a job. As I told you the first day you introduced yourself, the property is paid for, the permits are up to date and the inspections are either finished or arranged for."

She didn't appear to have a response.

"Never a dull day in the Hubrecht clan." Elise stood and started gathering plates and glasses from the table. She gave Emily a look that clearly said, *You plan to help?* but Emily shook her head and frowned at Donovan.

"So," Jacob interjected, "about the tree houses we saw on your website. Your blog said that a typical tree house takes a week and that you do small jobs between big projects?"

"Sometimes," Donovan allowed.

Jacob's eyes lit up.

"I didn't see any trees around here big enough for a tree house," Donovan remarked.

"Don't want a tree house, exactly," Jacob said. "Timmy and I were talking, and we want a child-size village, you know, with houses the size of small sheds, perfect for our guests in the age range of three to maybe twelve. Not just houses, mind you. We'd want a child-size fire station, a store, a movie theater, a school and a hospital. It could be a little bigger. Not only could Timmy and his soon-to-be little brother use it, but many of our guests bring children—"

"Whoa." Donovan appreciated the man's enthusiasm, but the picture he was painting would take a lot of time. Time Donovan didn't have. "I'm not sure you've thought about the real time and cost of such a project. I'm booked solid for the next two years. And if I do it when I have a free week, you'll be getting a new building once every six months, plus paying travel."

Donovan was now a week late on the Baer house, which was okay because he always calculated in extra time, but come the beginning of August, he was heading for California and his next job. Building a child-size village wasn't on the schedule. "Plus, you're a builder, too. You built this place."

"I was a lot younger then. And, I never did the detail you put into some of those houses. Timmy was quite impressed. I don't figure the cost would be much different than the tree house you made over in Colorado last year," Jacob said.

Donovan knew the exact one Jacob spoke of. It was connected to two trees, had two porches—front and back—and was made of cedar. Much bigger than a shed.

"I figure you'll charge me a little less, as it's easier to build on the ground rather than in a tree."

"You're still talking about five or six buildings," Donovan responded.

"Give me a ballpark figure, thinking maybe six structures?"

Donovan shook his head. "The tree houses are a passion of mine and I love building them. Unfortunately, I don't…"

Timmy's lips pursed, making him resemble his aunt from a few minutes ago.

"No." Jacob only said one word and Timmy stopped pouting.

Donovan figured this would be a good time to head for the buffet and fill his plate. When he returned, he quickly took a bite so he wouldn't have to say anything else right away. He thought about the offer. The tree houses weren't exactly what Donovan would call small jobs. They were intricate and had personality, and he wished he could build them full-time. Their owners, usually between the ages of six and sixteen, appreciated them in a way a wealthy seventy-something, like Baer, couldn't.

Jacob waited until Donovan's plate was almost empty before suggesting, "Could you maybe work in just two small houses between the end of this job and your next one? Emily is handy with a hammer. She's responsible for the good condition of our fencing and the remodels in the barn and bunkhouse. If she helped you, she might be able to finish the job."

"No." Emily sounded a lot like her dad.

No way did Donovan have time. But working with Emily…might prove very interesting. Maybe, just maybe, he could manage one.

Before any more discussion, Sam Miller walked in. He didn't look around, just headed to their table.

"Go find your mother," Jacob told Timmy. "Tell her we just might have an idea that works. Then, build me two houses out of Legos, so I can see your design ideas."

"Okay, Grandpa!"

Sam took Timmy's place, even going so far as to finish the lone cookie the boy left behind. From the look on his face, Donovan figured he'd need more than a cookie to put him in a good mood.

"Have you found out anything new?" Emily didn't wait for Sam to stop chewing.

"The medical examiner said there was no sign of trauma on our victim but his bones showed deterioration from arthritis. He thinks that'll make identification easier," Sam shared after swallowing. "He hasn't found proof that the man died from a stab wound, but he admits the skeleton has eroded so much that it might not be possible to establish the cause of death."

"How long has he been buried there? How old is he?"

"Nothing definite, but the ME thinks we have a Caucasian male who's been buried there for around thirty years, give or take a few, and who was between twenty-five and forty when he died." Sam never took his eyes off Jacob while he talked. Donovan glanced at Emily. She was oblivious, but Donovan wasn't. There was a reason Sam had shown up tonight, and it wasn't just to share details.

"The knife adds to the mystery." Sam continued watching Jacob. "Or, solves it. Good news is that it's not a generic knife found in any box or convenience store. It's hand tooled. We've been researching it and think we've found a match. Back in the sixties and seventies there was a family over in Wickenburg who had a silver and leather shop. They did quite well. The business fell apart, however, years later when the father died. They pretty much stopped making saddles and knives after that."

Sam pulled a photo from a folder he carried and held it out. The knife was stunning. Donovan knew good quality, even as tarnished as this knife was, when he saw it. There was some kind of stone near the handle, maybe ruby. Then there was a raised silver swirl design that stopped at the initials.

J.H.

"Maybe you've heard of the Rannik family. They made knives for a lot of carnivals, festivals, rodeos. I spoke with their youngest daughter. She is the last one working the trade, specializing in jewelry. She emailed me their client list, along with purchase dates and transactions. There was only one name I recognized."

It was the first time Donovan had witnessed Emily speechless. Jacob, for his part, paled a bit. Then, giving Sam a look that Donovan hoped he was never on the receiving end of, Jacob stood and left the room.

Emily got her voice back. "Of all the fool ideas, Sam. You know my father is not involved. He catches lizards and lets them go loose outside. He—"

"Had a life before he met your mother and started a family," Sam said quietly.

"He's an elder at our church."

Donovan knew that "our" church meant hers

as well as Sam's. The church he'd been invited to but hadn't attended.

"I don't like this either, Emily," Sam said, "but questioning is what I do. Right now, I'm just venturing out. It could be nothing."

"It is nothing." Jacob returned and tossed something on the table. It was a knife. The same knife as was in the baggy. Ruby, initials and all.

Only this knife wasn't tarnished.

Chapter Four

The Lost Dutchman Museum was on the edge of town, and Emily always came out on her days off. Sometimes she spent hours in the barn, working on the back section that was considered storage. She wanted to open it up to Apache Creek history, and she had enough pieces from the Majestic for one display that would appeal to people interested in both small-town and movie lore.

Just not John Wayne.

She also had remnants from Apache Creek's first church, school and post office. If she could talk the trustees into going to the city for more funding, she'd buy a few acres from the Pearl family. They owned most of the land around the museum. At one time, there'd been a Pearl Ranch. Now it was open space and for sale.

Emily hoped no one ever bought it.

Another reason she came in was to make sure everything was where it should be. Twice she'd

deterred tourists from breaking in to the barn
where exhibits were.

Even adults thought it okay to pull away boards
and pick or break locks just so they could see.
Once, she'd just missed a vandal who'd spray
painted graffiti on the barn housing a replica of
Jacob Waltz's cabin. The paint had still been wet!
Officer Sam Miller had filled out a report. She'd
repaired the damage.

Emily noted now how quiet the museum was
first thing in the morning. Usually she felt a little jog of excitement when she opened the door
and entered. Her world. She felt privileged and
amazed. How blessed she was to have a career
she loved. She cared for the past, brought history to life and made sure an imprint remained
for the future.

Today, the woven blankets and pieces of pottery didn't speak to her. The air in the museum
felt different, quiet and unassuming.

She was being ridiculous. And she knew it.
Turning on the lights, she adjusted the temperature and went around checking the exhibits. Nothing was out of place.

No, it was her life that had been trespassed on,
and she wasn't sure how to restore peace.

She walked through the aisles of the main
building, whispering prayers while straightening
photos and realigning displays. She did not believe

her dad had a connection with the body discovered last week. Still, her prayers felt ineffective.

Sometimes the present was more important than the future, especially when it involved her dad.

She'd made it through only one room when someone knocked at the front door. She ignored it. Hours were posted and she wasn't in the mood for giving a private tour. She didn't dare go to the window and try shooing a visitor away. For one thing, it felt rude. For another, twice when she'd done that it had been church members with family in town. Thus, the private tours.

Her phone buzzed. Taking it out, she checked the caller ID.

Elise's name displayed. She swiped her thumb across her phone to answer it, and said, "What's happening?"

"They've taken Dad in for questioning."

"I'll meet you at the police station." Emily turned, wanting to grab her purse from her desk drawer.

"Sam says it's routine. I'm on my way to be with him. Of course, he says he doesn't need me. Eva's handling everything here. Are you sure there's nothing you overlooked at the Baer place?"

"I'm sure, but I only looked at a certain perimeter where the body was found."

"Meaning?"

"Meaning I stayed within about one hundred and forty-four square feet."

"Paint me a picture."

"The size of your bedroom." Already, Emily was thinking ahead. She needed to look farther. The man had somehow arrived at his burial spot. He'd either walked or been carried. It would take a while, but she might be able to discover the path.

Yeah, right.

"I'm heading to the Baer house now," Emily promised, entering her office to grab her purse and then locking the door on her way out.

But as she stepped onto the front stoop, she found the one person she wasn't in the mood to see. Randall Tucker.

"I've been meaning to check out the museum. Any chance you could show me around?"

"I've an appointment. We open at nine tomorrow."

To his credit, he didn't brush past her and enter. Instead, he studied the building. Emily couldn't help herself. She looked, too. The exterior was roughly sawn ponderosa pine. The museum sign was lighter wood and the words *Lost Dutchman Museum* appeared to have been burned in.

Emily smiled. Her museum looked at home nestled against the backdrop of the Superstition Mountains. The barn distracted from it a bit, but the cook shanty to the left helped.

"This is a great location," Randall said. "You get much traffic?"

"We get plenty of traffic. We, however, are closed on Monday. Come back on a different day, and I'll show you around."

He scanned the main building. "Solid foundation. How old?"

"About fifty years. It was built in the sixties."

"Private or state?"

She'd learned a long time ago that losing her temper only made things worse. "When you come back, I'll get you a brochure. Or, you can go to the website. I update it every week." She gave one last tug on the door, making sure it was locked, and then headed for her truck.

On the drive to the Baer place, a good fifteen miles, she deliberately pushed Randall Tucker from her thoughts and focused on the events involving the body, in order.

She, along with Donovan, had been among the first to see the bones. He wasn't her first choice for a comrade, but he might do. She needed to talk to him some more because while she'd found the knife, it had been the medical examiner who declared the site a crime scene. Donovan, no doubt, had been present through every step.

She needed to talk to the medical examiner, too. She knew the man was a stickler for details and rarely missed a clue. Even though her perusal of the area turned up nothing else in the vicinity that might point to who the skeleton was and how he died, maybe the ME had noted something.

Besides the knife.

Nothing in the perimeter would vindicate her father. Yesterday, he hadn't been worried. "My word has always been truth," he said a dozen times at church. It was half a scripture. He was good at that.

She wondered if he was worried today.

She was, and she wasn't exactly sure why. She knew her father hadn't been involved in a murder.

Turning onto Main Street, she noted that the Miner's Lamp was doing a steady breakfast business. No doubt, the skeleton's discovery would give the people of Apache Creek something to talk about for weeks, maybe months.

Especially since suspicion had fallen, if only for a brief second, on her father.

Jacob Hubrecht, Emily thought as she drove past the park, still believed a handshake was binding. It had been decades since he'd lived outside Apache Creek. Before that, he'd been a bull rider, and she knew, having met most of his friends from those long-ago days, that they'd had their own code of honor.

A cowboy's handshake.

She didn't trust such casual contracts. She'd been across the United States, even working in South Dakota, where her job had been to return stolen artifacts to local tribes. Legislation claimed that it was necessary "to secure, for the present and future benefit of the American people, the protection of archaeological resources and sites which are on public lands and Indian lands." Yet, some of the most grievous offenders were fined in the three digits while they'd earned in the five digits from their stolen loot, no jail time or restoration.

The Natives called it erosion of justice.

She called it misplaced trust.

A handshake worked in her father's world, but just as the knife by the skeleton was eroded, so might be justice. This corpse was an intruder to George Baer, who thought a monstrosity of a house belonged on sacred soil.

The sign designating Ancient Trails Road was fairly new and looked out of place. She made a left and then slowed down so she could study the Baer house without anyone noticing. She no longer thought the soil so sacred.

Some secrets should stay buried.

Two trucks were parked where a driveway would one day be. Emily recognized one as belonging to John Westerfield, who had been out of work for almost two years. He'd have probably shown up even if they'd found a mass grave. The rest of Donovan's crew appeared to be missing. She knew Smokey quite well. It would be a while before he ventured back.

The other truck was Donovan's.

She edged her foot onto the gas and then braked, slowing, suddenly sure that driving out here was the wrong thing to do. She'd wanted to shut the construction down, but not this way.

Unfortunately, Donovan stepped out the front door, giving her no choice but to park, exit her truck and head for the house he was building.

"Everything okay?" For the most part, their paths had been crossing via controversy, but Donovan—thanks to his ex-fiancée, Olivia—knew how to recognize a damsel in distress.

Olivia had perfected the art; Emily not so much.

"I hope so," she managed. "My dad's at the station for questioning."

"I'm sorry to hear that. So strange that there would be two knives. Did your dad ever remember how he came to have that one?"

"Right after you left. It was his prize for finaling in a Prescott Rodeo."

Donovan nodded, thinking it made perfect sense. "You want to come in? I'll show you the guts of this place. It's not as bad as you make it out to be."

She shook her head. "I've seen this house a million times, usually in a gated community on an upscale street in a big city."

"You haven't seen this house," Donovan protested. "It's one of a kind, and I designed it."

She looked at the Baer house again. He did, too,

pleased with what he saw. Even without the doors, windows and cabinets in place yet, he could visualize how they'd complement his creation.

He was bringing his drawings to life.

"A million times," she muttered. As if to prove her point, she questioned, "Two-car garage with a workshop attached?"

"Yes."

"Four bedrooms, each with its own bath?"

"Yes." Now he was getting annoyed.

"A study and dining room?"

Had she seen his plans? "Yes."

"I forget anything besides the kitchen and family room?" she queried.

"Baer specifically asked for a hallway that would serve as a gallery."

"Ah," she quipped, "that must be the custom part."

"The arrangement, proportions and style make it custom. Plus, when we finish with the landscape…"

She pointed behind him. He turned, seeing the Superstition Mountains in all their glory.

"You can't compete with that," she said simply.

"I don't want to. I just want Baer to be able to sit on his back porch and enjoy the view."

"The view he's wrecking."

Ah, now the Emily Hubrecht who'd first approached him was totally back.

"This house is not on a hill. There are no

neighbors for miles. He's not infringing on any-one's view."

"You mentioned style. What style would you call your design?"

He answered without thinking, because he knew the style and had answered the question a million times. "French Country."

"French Country in Arizona. That's different."

"It's what Baer wanted."

For a moment, he thought she'd protest. Then she nodded before following him through the door. "Big" was all she said, walking through the foyer and living area to the kitchen. "And there will just be two people living here?"

"Just two."

She shook her head, sitting in a camp chair while Donovan pulled a bottle of water out of a small cooler. She took a long drink. "This house could be made of gold, and I wouldn't like it. Until you showed up with your plans and permits, my life was perfect."

"Perfect? I don't think anyone's life is perfect."

"My life's not perfect now."

He decided to give her a break and change the subject. "If you know the exact rodeo, can you find out if someone else finaled, maybe in a dif-ferent event, and had the same initials?"

"We hope. Sam is checking. I guess they want to authenticate it. See if it's the knife made for my dad by the Rannik company. Both knives that is."

"Who did the initials?" Donovan asked.

"They did, at least on Dad's. He says it's common for a company to have a booth right at a rodeo event."

"That's good. Because it means anyone could have purchased the knife and asked for the same initials. Not just the winners."

"The difference is Dad's knife also has the logo of the rodeo branded into the handle."

"Does the one we found have the logo?" Donovan thought about the mound of dirt no longer cordoned off but still as the medical examiner left it.

Her sudden look made him rethink what he'd said.

We.

It wasn't the word but how he'd said it. Making them more or less a team.

"Sam won't tell us." For a moment, she thought Donovan was going to scoot his chair closer, reach out for her. That was silly. He was the enemy. If not for this house, there'd be no body and no knife.

She shook her head a little harder than she meant to. Those kinds of thoughts did no good. "Dad having that knife physically in his possession was really…" Her words tapered off. She didn't know how to finish. Her dad wasn't under suspicion, not really, especially for a crime where there were no witnesses and the body hadn't even been identified.

"Amazing," Donovan said. "And all because the home owner decided he wanted to add a circular driveway."

Around him the house loomed, like a monster ready to engulf whatever got in its way, whether land or human.

After a moment, when she didn't respond, he queried, "Museum closed today?"

Emily nodded. "It's closed every Sunday and Monday. Monday because of numbers and Sunday for a day of rest."

He arched an eyebrow.

"Do you work on Sunday?" she asked.

"If I need to."

"Did you work yesterday? I didn't see you at church."

He laughed, but she caught something in his eyes, maybe sadness. "You've never seen me at church. I don't attend."

"Did you ever?" This was not the conversation she meant to have. She was here to look for clues.

He took a long gulp of his water before answering, "Yes, a long time ago I went to church. Why are you asking?"

"It was at church that I found out you were building this house."

"You mean people were praying for me before I even arrived?"

"No, more like people were talking about you. I heard about it from your mailman."

"That's a first. I don't think I've received any mail here."

"It was added to his route. He mentioned it to me and said he'd driven by this lot after delivering mail nearby. I almost fell out of the pew when he described some builder out at Ancient Trails Road already making decisions about where to put utilities, a septic system and driveway."

"Still not doing so well with driveways," Donovan mourned.

"And I am not doing so well in stopping you." She'd offered God a dozen apologies throughout that day because after what the mailman shared, she'd not heard a word of the sermon.

Emily had lost valuable time. The land had already been sold and paid for, making her protests too little and too late. Donovan Russell had been a brick wall when it came to reason.

She'd always been more of a husky, taking hold and shaking until she got her way. And she hated losing.

"You've stopped me now. I still don't have a full crew and I've been advised to leave the area around the grave alone, just in case it's a crime scene."

"That's why I'm here." She finished her water and stood. "I want to see if there's anything I missed."

He stood, too, but didn't move toward the door.

"I don't think there's as much as a rock left. They bagged everything."

"I want to see if I can figure how he got there—"

Donovan finished her sentence. "Vehicle, animal, footprints or shoe marks."

"Yes," she said slowly.

"They did all that."

"What did they decide?"

"That they agreed with your original assessment that the body had been here more than thirty years."

"I really wish it had been here two hundred and thirty years."

"Life's not always fair."

Emily wasn't telling Donovan something he didn't already know.

He followed her back through the living room and foyer and out to the crime scene. Except for the cordon tape and markers, it was just a hole.

"I'd think it was ready for a hot tub if it wasn't in the front yard," Donovan tried to joke.

She, apparently, didn't think he was funny.

"So, what are we going to do first?" he queried. She didn't answer, just stood looking down at where the skeleton used to be.

The whole thing spooked Donovan somewhat. He just wished he could, in good conscience, fill the hole back in. Without meaning to, he stepped too close to the edge of the hole so a few kernels of dirt fell back into the grave.

Emily's eyes grew big.

"What?"

"I can't help but think of Ecclesiastes and 'the dust returns to the ground it came from, and the spirit returns to God who gave it.'"

He nodded, thinking she was a whole lot more connected to the earth and to family than he was.

"Just think," she said softly, "some mother, wife, sister, daughter, might be waiting for the return of a man who no longer lives. He's been buried in this shallow grave and forgotten." She never ceased to surprise him. Compassion was a trait he knew he needed to develop.

"The only clue to his identity," she continued, "a knife that looks identical to one my father owns, down to the initials."

"A knife your father still has," Donovan reminded her. It somewhat amazed him that their roles had switched, and now he wanted to stop work and help her. The woman whose job it was to ruin his day, either by producing a five-page petition with the names of Apache Creek residents who didn't want their view marred by a minimansion, or by going to her knees next to what could have been the ancient bones of a Native American, claiming there might be more and gloating that she'd be here a long time.

He almost wished it had been a Native American skeleton. Then, her father wouldn't be under suspicion.

"It will be like looking for a needle in a haystack," she muttered.

"Hey, I grew up on a dairy farm in Mytal, Nebraska. I know a lot about haystacks. I know which cow needs to maintain her weight, and where to spread the hay, and—" For the past two months, she'd been a thorn in his side always ready to battle. He liked that Emily better. This dejected one was out of character. Still, his attempt to encourage her didn't seem to be working.

Her expression was so serious that he knew he had to help. It surprised him, the sudden need. "I watched the authorities all last week. I know where they looked and where they didn't."

It took her a moment. He watched as she inhaled, a big breath that seemed to fill her. Then she drew herself up to her full height and nodded. "Let's do it."

John Westerfield chose that moment to make the mistake of coming outside to see what they were doing. Donovan should have texted him and warned, *Avoid front of house until I call you.*

"You can help," Emily informed John, running to her truck and retrieving trash bags that she quickly handed out.

"She's always been a bit high maintenance," John said.

Donovan believed him. For the next two hours, they walked a square mile, what Emily called a grid, slowly. She told them to pick up anything that didn't belong, anything suspicious. He doubted the old shoe, candy wrappers, beer can or piece of tire he'd stowed in his garbage bag was going to help.

John's contribution was a page from an old newspaper, ripped in half, and a dozen bullet casings, which he wanted to keep.

Her cache wasn't much better. She also had candy wrappers, plus ten beer cans, what appeared to be a section of tarp and thirty-five cents.

Still, she looked quite happy.

When she drove away, he realized he'd only seen her smile twice, when she first saw the bones and now leaving with her trash.

He slowly walked back to the Baer house. He understood ceramic tile more than he did women.

Tuesday morning, Emily got to the museum early. She had a lot to do. At the trustees meeting, she'd been encouraged to plan some kind of activity to get people to the museum, similar to the library's celebration of its sixtieth birthday this coming Saturday.

She knew for a fact that the library had more funding than she did—maybe because they made money on overdue books.

She also knew that unless she got more private funding, the museum would be in danger of closing down. Her biggest enemy was its location. The Lost Dutchman Museum was part of eighty acres of land and only this tiny portion had been donated to the city. The rest belonged to the Pearl Ranch, and Emily didn't know the Pearl who still owned the land. He or she didn't live in Apache Creek, hadn't in decades.

After walking the museum's main room and ascertaining that all was well, she sat at her computer and researched other museums in Arizona. Comparatively, she curated at a very small one. Most of the museums that had special events were bigger, and in every case those events called for bringing exhibits from other museums in. The Lost Dutchman Museum was so tiny that lending a small Salado bowl was really something. She'd only be able to ask for something small in return.

That wouldn't generate visitors.

If she were to have some sort of event, it had to be museum themed.

Unlocking the door, she flipped the sign to Open and wished there were a line waiting.

Back at her computer, she checked emails. Some were from college students who'd been passed her name by their professors. She answered a few questions and for the others, she provided names of people who could help.

Two people queried about job openings.

She managed not to laugh.

The Heard Museum sent her a photo of her Salado bowl. It looked lost among the others being displayed.

At the end of more than three dozen emails came a query that surprised her. In the United States there were very few museums that centered only on Native American artifacts. Her final email was from the curator at the Native American Heritage Museum, asking if she was looking for work and included a job description that advertised a salary three times larger than what she was making in Apache Creek.

Not wanting to be rude, she sent a thank-you.

Not even for three times the money did she intend to move. Apache Creek was in her blood, and her blood lived in Apache Creek.

With that, she looked up and smiled at the museum's first visitor of the day.

Six hours later, at four, she closed and locked the door. On the computer, she filled in the daily accounts, entering the number of visitors, what souvenirs sold—the Lost Dutchman Gold Map was the top seller, followed by pens shaped like a pickax—and her hours.

Then she headed home.

"You working the floor tonight?" Elise queried her at the front desk. Emily's whole life she'd walked through a dude ranch front desk and down a hallway to where the family lived. The family was getting smaller, though, with Eva, and soon Elise, moving.

Granted, both weren't moving far.

"Yes."

"I rented out two of the cabins as well as one of the rooms. I expect we'll be a little busier tonight. Did Sam call and say if anything you found yesterday while walking the Baer place was helpful?"

"No, he hasn't called."

Elise shook her head. "I spent a long time talking with Cook. He has no clue if he attended the Prescott Rodeo all those years ago. He says they all blur together after a while."

"Probably for Dad, too. What year would that have been? Did Dad remember?"

"He says nineteen seventy-eight or nine."

"Sounds about right. Dad would have been in his twenties." Emily took off down the hallway. On each side were photos. A few were of a twenty-something Jacob. Her favorite showed him on a horse in full gallop heading for the camera. His hat was on, but you could see his longish hair breezing from the sides. He leaned forward slightly. His face was mostly in shadow, but no one could fail to notice its beauty.

She'd said that once to her dad, almost to the very word.

Men aren't beautiful, he'd responded.

Mom thought you were beautiful, Eva had piped up. If Emily remembered, that had been the year

Eva went off to the university, driving back and forth every day to Tempe because she couldn't bear to leave the ranch.

Elise and Emily were a little more willing to spread their wings, but both had flown back.

In a matter of minutes, Emily was out of her museum shirt and khakis and into her blue Lost Dutchman Ranch shirt and jeans with a black apron tried around her waist.

The dining room was at the back of the main house. Picnic tables held guests, visitors and employees. The atmosphere was meant to be fun and relaxed. They did not serve a four-star meal. Tonight's menu was barbecue pork, beans and potato chips. All homemade by Cook, who'd traveled with Jacob on the rodeo and retired at an early age to work at the Lost Dutchman. His specialty was Mexican food, but actually there wasn't a food type he couldn't produce.

Meals were served buffet style with only one server walking around, taking orders, and making sure all the guests had what they needed.

At the back of the restaurant was a game room, mostly a kids' area, complete with a television for watching movies or playing video games. This late in June, as hot as it was, they didn't get many kids.

An hour into her shift, Emily's cell sounded. She took it out and checked the screen: Jane de la Rosa. Looking around, she noted her dad sitting at his favorite table with one of the families who'd checked in today—strangers becoming friends—and Jilly Greenhouse, who lived in the house closest to the Lost Dutchman Ranch. Ducking into the kids' game room, she answered.

"You'll never guess! Never," Jane said.

"Aren't you working?"

"Yes, though we're pretty slow tonight." Jane worked at the Miner's Lamp, the rustic restaurant in town. It had been around even longer than the Lost Dutchman Ranch.

"What do you want me to guess?"

"I waited on a man tonight. He's still here. He's an EPA inspector out of Phoenix—don't ask me what EPA stands for—who came to check some sort of levels at the Baer house."

"Okay…" Emily tried to figure why this was news. Since the groundbreaking, Donovan had had one inspector after another at the Baer place.

"Well, I heard this guy on the phone. I guess the levels of something called radon gas were high."

"And that's bad?" Emily queried.

"Bad enough that when Donovan called Baer with the news, Baer apparently said to halt construction."

"For how long?"

"Maybe for good," Jane said. "The inspector was on the phone with his boss. He sounded a bit surprised. I'm wondering if Baer's getting fed up.

I mean first it's you protesting, then it's a skeleton and now this."

Emily should have felt elated, should have jumped for joy, but all she could picture was the brown-haired man who'd walked in the hot sun for hours picking up an old shoe and plenty of beer cans just because she'd asked him to.

Chapter Five

Donovan called it a day. Even with the evac cooler, it was too hot to do much more than complain. It annoyed Donovan that he, out of everyone, did most of the complaining about the heat.

The floors were scheduled for next week; he'd call to reschedule. Surely Baer would come to his senses soon. There wasn't a house in Apache Creek that didn't have radon levels. The inspector had even taken the phone and spoken to Baer personally.

But George Baer said to wait. And, Donovan heard something in the man's voice that hadn't been there before. A subtle annoyance, the slapping of hands, sounding very much like a silent *I'm done*.

Donovan very much wanted to be done. He wanted to get back to the life he'd planned for himself: traveling, building the types of structures he wanted to build, adventure. But the phone call he'd made to Nolan Tate hadn't changed Donovan's situation. According to Tate, there was no place to put Donovan, so he could just wait.

Great. Every day he worked for Nolan Tate was one step closer to paying his debt to the man. Being out of work meant no debt eliminated and Donovan working for the man longer than he wanted to.

Turning on the camper's generator, he stepped inside, shed his clothes and hopped into the tiny shower.

Looking for evidence had been hot and tiring. Emily hadn't been bothered by the heat at all. She'd managed to look as if being outdoors, slow roasted, was an everyday occurrence. He'd checked the weather in California, the location of his next scheduled job if Tate didn't change his mind. If everything worked out, Donovan would be there at the end of July, beginning of August, about the time Apache Creek, Arizona, went from slow roast to extreme grill.

And there was nothing else for Donovan to do for over a month until the California project.

He wanted to laugh. It was almost too funny. He'd had to take this job with Baer, had compromised his talent for money and now was stuck in small-town Arizona living in his camper.

He'd need to find an RV park soon, now that he was no longer employed. June in Apache Creek, that shouldn't be a problem. Snowbirds—those who sojourned in this part of Arizona because of the mild winter weather—didn't start arriving until late September or early October.

The next few phone calls were hard to make. Donovan could employ John until the end of the week. Tate Luxury Homes didn't leave a mess behind. Helping with cleanup wasn't fun, and John didn't take it well.

Smokey answered on the third ring and said he already had a new job offer for him and his cousins.

All that Donovan had left to do was take care of himself. No way did he want to go weeks without money coming in, and if he wasn't supervising a job, he wasn't getting a paycheck.

Donovan hesitated a moment—after all, the man he was about to call had spent part of the previous morning being interrogated by the police. Jacob Hubrecht might not be in the best of moods.

"You calling to find out what happened at the police station?" Jacob said immediately after hello.

"No, Emily was here recently. She kept me informed."

"Did she tell you that, without knowing the identity of the body and time of death, the only questions asked of me were 'What else can you tell us about the knife?' and 'Were you ever in the vicinity where the body was discovered?'"

"No."

"Only thing I could tell the cops was that the wife and I often rode horses in the area after we first married."

"She did tell me a bit about that."

While they'd walked the Baer property, she'd painted a picture of Jacob and Naomi Hubrecht that sounded too good to be true: young, in love, doing everything together.

Donovan looked from the camper's window at the almost-complete Baer home and tried to imagine a young couple on horseback, riding the land just because they wanted to.

He'd had a horse up until junior high; Risky Business had been his best friend. Then, about the time Risky developed laminitis, Donovan discovered sports and girls.

Funny, Donovan had locked away the memory of Risky Business, preferring to remember all the things he didn't like about growing up on a dairy farm. He didn't particularly want a good memory to surface now.

It didn't belong in his life today.

"I'm looking for a job," Donovan said, thinking about the months he might go without a paycheck.

"Emily said something about radon gas levels being high."

Donovan closed his eyes. Already the whole town knew. "Yes, Baer's halted construction for a while." Donovan purposely made it sound like a temporary stoppage. "I've a month, maybe a month and a half, to devote to your Tinytown."

"Good to know. Draw up a contract and let's get started."

"Monday soon enough?"

Ending the call, Donovan knew of at least one person besides Jacob who benefitted from Baer's withdrawal but for a different reason. Emily Hubrecht. Donovan hoped she didn't gloat too much.

Emily shook her head at the crowded parking lot. Why couldn't the museum have a day like this? Just a little after seven in the morning, and the parking lot was full. Gathering up her storyteller bag, she walked two blocks before reaching her destination. It looked as if the library's sixtieth birthday with a morning full of both indoor and outdoor festivities had drawn a crowd. Emily checked her watch as she strolled up the sidewalk. It was just a quarter after. The festival had started fifteen minutes ago and was already going full steam.

"Hey, Emily!" Eva had left the house early this morning. Her husband, Jesse, had come along to help set up a Native American loom so Eva could put on a live demonstration. She was dressed in a burnt-red manta, a plain cotton dress with a decorative, beaded belt around her protruding belly and moccasins. One of Eva's blankets was today's top raffle prize—all proceeds going to the library.

"Hi, Emily!" Jane de la Rosa was in a booth a little ways down from Eva, selling green eggs and ham inspired by Dr. Seuss. This was, after all, a library event. Jane wore a red floppy hat. Not for the first time, Emily wished Jane would find someone, settle down and have a dozen kids. She was a natural-born mother. The line in front of her was ten deep, and the picnic tables were full.

Behind the library, in a vacant lot, Emily's father drove a tractor hitched to a wagon stocked with just enough hay bales for seats. The town's librarian, Lydia Hamm, had asked him to dress up like a classic storybook cowboy. She'd been thinking Sheriff Woody from *Toy Story*. He arrived in jeans and a long-sleeved shirt. Lydia probably forgave him because, along with a red neckerchief, he wore cowboy boots and a dusty Stetson. He'd stay until the crowd waned, then head home because he'd left Elise alone at the ranch.

On the other side of the library, where there were no booths, a scavenger hunt was just beginning. Emily checked her watch. She had thirty minutes before story hour, and she knew exactly what she was going to say. Setting her bag of props on the ground against a tree, she went over to Timmy and said, "You need any help?"

"I'm in second grade," he answered indignantly. Still, he showed her a list.

1. A Feather—honoring *The Indian in the Cup-board*
2. A Bag of Potato Chips—honoring *The Very Hungry Caterpillar*
3. Something Round and Orange—honoring *James and the Giant Peach*
4. A Mirror—honoring *Sleeping Beauty*
5. A Stuffed Beaver—honoring *The Lion, the Witch and the Wardrobe*
6. A Wand—honoring *Harry Potter*
7. A Packet of Seeds—honoring *The Secret Garden*

"I promise, after the scavenger hunt, I'll come listen to your story."

"What do you win if you find everything?" a familiar voice asked from behind her.

Emily turned to find Donovan Russell. She hadn't even heard his approach. Now he leaned over, checking out Timmy's list.

"I get to pick one of the books," Timmy announced.

"So," Donovan queried, "you might get a copy of *The Secret Garden*?"

"No. I want *The Lion, the Witch and the Wardrobe*. Eva says I'll like it."

"You will," Donovan agreed.

"You've read it?" Emily questioned.

"Yes, but I liked *The Great Divorce* more."

"I don't like divorce," Timmy said, and Emily gave Donovan a look that said *Don't go there*.

The whistle blew, indicating the start of the hunt. Timmy shot them a look, letting them know they'd delayed him, and then took off running.

"I didn't expect to see you here," Emily said as she went to retrieve her bag.

Donovan didn't follow. Emily turned and watched as he read the scavenger-hunt list aloud to a little girl too young to decipher the words. When he joined her, he said, "I closed the Baer place yesterday, and I don't start working for your father until Monday—that is, if he agrees to the contract. I've got a free weekend."

"I'm sorry…" She wasn't quite sure what to say. She wasn't sorry the job shut down, but she was sorry that it affected Donovan. If not for where he built and his not respecting why he shouldn't build there, she could almost like him.

Almost.

"It's not the first time my plans have changed," Donovan said.

She nodded, hoping she didn't look smug about what had happened at the Baer place. Radon gas was not how she wanted to halt building. "Once the mystery surrounding the body is solved, I'm heading out to Ancient Trails Road. I want to poke around a bit, outside the Baer property, to see what I can find."

"We didn't find a single artifact," Donovan reminded her.

"You wouldn't know an arrowhead if it bit you."

Donovan laughed. "There were other biting things to worry about."

She laughed, too, liking the way the sun made his brown hair a tad golden, the way his eyes crinkled and how she had to look up at him. "My dad's thrilled that you'll get to work on Tinytown."

"I'm looking forward to it, too."

Together, they walked around the last few booths, one for used books and the others for arts and crafts.

"Why don't you have a booth?" he asked after a few minutes of companionable silence.

"What?"

"Advertising the museum."

"You mean the museum you've never visited?"

"Ouch." He put a hand over his heart. "In my defense, I've been busy. Who's working it today?"

"I'll head over there once I'm done here. I've a sign on the door telling any tourists—there's not many in June—that I'll be back at noon and advising them to come here and enjoy themselves."

"The curator's 'gone fishing' ploy?"

"You can look at it that way," she agreed.

"You still didn't answer my question about why you don't have a booth."

"What would I do? The artifacts are too valuable to bundle up and bring over here. I could hand out brochures, but people would just throw them away."

"What's in your museum?"

She was a bit annoyed that he didn't know. "We've the traditional arts and crafts, centuries-old artifacts, tools and such. We also have an exhibit on Jacob Waltz, the original Lost Dutchman. We've old prospector paraphernalia like spur rowels, drilling steel and one of my favorite pieces, a Spanish crossbow dart."

Donovan nodded. "So, what you do is set up a gold-panning exhibit. Let the kids pan for fool's gold. Tell them the history while they're engaged. Let them keep some of what they pan. Make sure that whatever you store it in has the museum's name, hours and even a discount coupon to be used during the hottest months."

Emily bit back her surprise. "What? You have a degree in marketing?"

"A minor. I'm into building and selling homes. You better believe I know how to make a sale. Doesn't matter if it's a tangible product or a tourist tr—"

She gave him credit; he'd stopped himself from saying *tourist trap*.

"Or a tourist's cultural landmark."

"It's an idea," she agreed. "Too bad the library probably won't celebrate its sixty-first birthday."

She opened the library's front door, feeling the air-conditioning and smelling the sweet aroma of books. She'd spent a lot of her childhood here. She'd read all the *Ramona* books, sometimes sitting on one of the beanbag chairs in the children's section. She would reread the parts featuring Ramona's mother and dream about her own mother. Those were her favorites. Sometimes she'd go back in time with *Little House on the Prairie*. Ma was a wealth of wisdom. It hadn't occurred to Emily until she was in high school that none of the books she read had Native American families, Native American mothers.

She'd started writing one but never got past page ten because her imagination always seemed inclined to have the mother die.

She couldn't write that storyline.

Couldn't seem to get away from it, either.

So, she started reading Native American textbooks, biographies and history books. She couldn't create fiction, but she could research fact.

Today she was a hundred pages into her family's history. Of course, the book had taken a turn and included much of Apache Creek's history.

Donovan put his hand on her shoulder. "You going to stand here, in the way, or enter?"

"Oh."

She clutched her bag closer and headed for the bathroom, where she could change. Storytelling was an art form. Her big sister Eva had the loom. Elise had her riding skills. For Emily, it was both the spoken and written word.

When she finally exited the bathroom, attired in a black cotton dress with a yellow beaded belt and yellow boots, the children's room was full. Timmy was in the front row, his welcoming smile displaying some missing teeth, with three of his best friends surrounding him. Her audience seemed to range from newborns to eighty-year-olds. Didn't matter. Her plan for today involved toddlers to primary school students. After all, they were in the children's section.

"Aliksa'i," she greeted.

"That means 'most wonderful,'" Timmy informed the ground. "It also means 'we're about to begin.'"

Emily opened her bag, took out ten ears of corn and gave them to Timmy to hand out. Then, she sat cross-legged on the floor in front of the children. Most scooted forward, some reaching to touch her clothes, especially the rainbow-colored dance scarf. She gently guided a few questing fingers away.

"This ceremonial dress belongs to my sister, not me. She shares it with the understanding that I'll take care of it. Has anyone ever trusted you with something?"

The answers came quickly.

"I'm trusted to not break my mom's cell phone."

"I'm trusted to help put in DVDs for my little sister to watch."

That got a follow-up response.

"I'm trusted to turn off YouTube if it's something my gramma wouldn't watch."

Looking around the room, at each laughing face, her gaze settled on the only person in the room who wasn't a child, parent or grandparent.

"What are you trusted with, Donovan?"

He paused only a moment before responding, "I'm trusted with not interrupting the storyteller."

It was the perfect opening. "Corn has always been important in the Southwest. It was a main food crop. How many of you love popcorn?"

Emily taught them how to make a popcorn popping noise, modeling soft versus loud. Then, she wove the story of the Corn Maiden. As she spoke, she introduced hand gestures for more audience participation. In the middle, they sang a song that necessitated the beating of a drum. Half the boys pounded on their knees, the other half received rattles. The girls moved their hands and fingers, pretending to be butterflies. Standing, she danced around them, careful not to step on any tiny feet or fingers, and held a mask up to her face.

Donovan watched her every move. It was a heady feeling having him there. It made her feel graceful, feminine, appreciated. Not what a storyteller needed but definitely what a woman needed.

Then, sitting down once more, she took the last object from her bag and carefully unwrapped it. Holding it up, she made sure everyone could see her kachina.

"The corn maidens were not meant to belong to man, so legend says that they were disguised as kachinas so man would not recognize them."

"That kachina is not big enough to be mistaken for a real person," Isabella Hamm pointed out.

"Of course not," Emily agreed. "I'm telling a story. One that's been passed down for centuries. You are honored by getting to hear it."

"Did your dad tell it to you?"

"No, one of my uncles did. And now I tell the story to you."

Timmy instigated the applause, ever his youngest aunt's biggest fan. Emily nodded, answered a few questions and then started gathering her props before standing and looking to the back of the room for Donovan.

He was no longer a part of her audience.

She didn't like the disappointed feeling that swept over her.

Donovan stepped from the library, found a quiet corner and listened as once again Nolan Tate insisted there was no work until the job started in California at the end of next month.

Donovan wasn't surprised when Nolan hung up without saying goodbye. The man was angry. His only daughter had been set to marry Donovan. Nolan had spent tens of thousands of dollars booking the country club, caterers and photographers, as well as buying his daughter and her groom a home.

Olivia hadn't liked the house her daddy purchased. She wanted to live in the home she'd grown up in. So, her daddy prepared to move.

When Donovan said he preferred to choose a house and pay for it themselves, Nolan laughed.

So did Olivia.

Just six months before the wedding, Donovan knew he was in trouble. Now, he was paying his almost father-in-law back for the down payments as well as money borrowed when Donovan first joined Tate Luxury Homes. The agreement was done under the guidance of the company's lawyer. It was the only way Donovan could keep his reputation as well as his honor, since he'd called off the wedding.

"Donovan!" Jacob Hubrecht came around the library corner just as Donovan slipped the phone into his back pocket. "Good to see you here."

"I closed down the Baer place yesterday. Got the paperwork turned in this morning." Checking his watch, Donovan continued, "I'm planning to visit the Apache Creek Desert Oasis in a while to see if I can rent a spot for a month and a half. I don't think it will be a problem."

"That's right," Jacob said. "You're living in an RV. Guess I hadn't considered that you'd need to move off the Baer place. Why don't you park the RV behind my barn and I'll put you up in one of the cabins? We're seldom full in the summer. Consider it part of your pay for building Tinytown."

"You don't have—"

"I know I don't have to. It's just a sensible solution. Think—you won't need to worry about meals or travel. You'll finish faster. You did say your next job starts next month, right? In California?"

"Palmdale," Donovan agreed. "I guess it does make sense. You mind if I head over later today?"

"I'll tell Eva. Come on."

What Donovan really wanted to do was head back into the library and catch the rest of Emily's storytelling. There was something about a woman dancing around two dozen children that made him want to see more.

He caught up to Jacob, who was already standing a few feet from Eva. They waited while she explained her technique to three little girls who were clearly itching to get their fingers on the yarn. "You know, everything you suggested was American small town. Why don't we do something to celebrate Emily's heritage? We could build a tepee or hogan…"

Jacob frowned. "It's a fine idea, but you'd have to square that with Emily or even one of my brothers-in-law."

"Dad, aren't you still doing the hayride?"

"Cooper took over to give me a break. We'll probably be at it a while longer."

The three girls in front of Eva stood up. "Bye, Miss Eva."

"Speaking of needing a break." Eva reached out for her father so he could help her up. "Kneeling for hours while nine months pregnant isn't much fun."

"Your mother said the same thing."

A look passed between the two, something that tugged at Donovan's heart. Clearly Jacob's wife had been loved and was still missed.

"I ran into Donovan," Jacob said. "He's bringing his RV over this afternoon. We're going to put him up in one of the cabins while he builds Tinytown."

"Oh, Timmy will be thrilled. Where is he, by the way? I've not seen him for a good hour."

Donovan spoke up. "He was just in Emily's story time. She gave a talk about the Corn Maiden."

Jacob's eyes twinkled. "Her mother's stories. Emily's pestered both Eva and her uncles since she was little. Now she knows more than anyone else. She's passing them down. There was a time she was writing them, but that girl's got more on her plate than a casserole at a church potluck."

"I don't bring them to life like Emily does. She's always been a storyteller." Eva, hands on her back, paced back and forth. "She could spin a tale. Got her in trouble more than once. In kindergarten, she pulled another little girl's hair and then told her teacher that Coyote made her do it."

"Coyote?"

Eva grinned. "The Trickster. In Hopi legends, he causes all kinds of trouble. Hang around Emily enough, you'll know them all."

"Not just the Hopi legends got that girl in trouble," Jacob added. "She got quite a few ideas from Harold Mull, our foreman. You'll meet him later today. In first grade, during recess, she stuck a bunch of little rocks in her mouth. Whoever was on recess duty told her to spit them out, and she wouldn't. By the time I got to the school, she was in the principal's office, tears streaming down her cheeks, and tired of all the small rocks in her mouth but too stubborn to spit them out."

"Harold," Eva continued, "told her that if she were ever thirsty, to just suck on stone. Apparently, the recess teacher wouldn't let her go in for a drink, and Emily decided to take care of the issue in a unique way."

"I paid for the installation of drinking fountains outside," Jacob said. "Don't know why they weren't there already. This is Arizona."

By the time Donovan left Eva and Jacob, story hour was over and Emily was gone. Leaving Donovan feeling that he'd once again fallen victim to a missed opportunity.

Chapter Six

Emily left the library festival a good twenty minutes later than she meant to. She had nobody to blame but herself. She'd hurried out of Elise's clothes and went looking for Donovan.

She didn't find him.

Probably, she told herself when she left Main Street and aimed her truck for the museum, he was holed up in some corner with his cell phone. Sometimes, she wished the device had never been invented. Other times, like when she needed it to find an out-of-the-way address, she thought it a better invention than ketchup.

She pushed Donovan from her thoughts—it took the entire drive—and pulled into the museum's empty parking lot.

She wished just one car waited for her, a happy family hoping to explore the past. One that wouldn't even care that her note specified her return time and that she was a solid thirty minutes late.

"Should have grabbed some green eggs and ham to go," she muttered to herself, taking down the notice and flipping the sign to Open. She stashed her bag in her office. No way did she want something to happen to her kachina or Elise's things. Then she settled her purse in the cabinet up front.

Before she could do one more thing, her stomach growled.

She'd settle for what she had in the employee office, which came with a small refrigerator and a microwave. A moment later she finished a banana, followed by five crackers and a bottle of water. Times like these, she wished the museum gift area was more than just a few items for sale by the cashier. A candy bar would be perfect just now.

Of course, that would add one more job description to her already-full agenda: curator, cleaning staff, accountant, cashier.

She turned on the lights, adjusted the temperature and went around checking the exhibits. Today as she walked, her prayers were focused on giving God praise for what He was doing with the library. She thanked Him also for the attentive children who'd been so taken with her story. Then, she segued to her family, especially Eva, who'd looked so cute, so very pregnant, kneeling before the loom. Emily ended with a prayer request for the museum and its future.

When it was winter, she actually had volunteers helping out. The snowbirds donated a few hours a week to welcoming visitors and walking them around. Emily did maintenance, caught up on record keeping and wrote.

June through September, she was alone.

Still, she was doing better than her predecessor. He'd worked the museum for twenty-five years and not one thing had changed.

The barn had been storage for junk. What a waste of space.

She had a dozen ideas, but no budget and even less time. What she really wanted was to stop waitressing at the Lost Dutchman Ranch unless her family was truly in a pinch. But the money she made there enabled her to pay her bills and pretty much do what she needed to do—like attend the Native American History Conferences and buy items for the museum. It gave her time to write articles that challenged how Native American history was represented in museums around the United States.

Sitting down at the front desk, she stared through the door that led to the main room and thought, *This is my museum. I will make it the best it can be.*

She just needed more visitors and the funds to do more than pay the bills. She turned on the computer and went right to email. Her last report to the board showed they were not running on a deficit. Thankfully, the Lost Dutchman Museum was not a million-dollar structure with high costs. The city of Apache Creek owned the building and land outright. If not for the museum's high electricity costs, they'd turn a profit. Still, at least one board member, Darryl Feeney, argued that the number of visitors kept dwindling and the electricity bill kept escalating.

Right now, Emily's biggest fear was they'd close the museum in the summer and only open for the winter. If that happened, she'd become a part-time employee.

"I need an endowment," she muttered.

The words had barely left her lips when a truck pulled into the parking lot.

Donovan Russell.

Emily stood and made sure no cracker crumbs peppered her dark blue Lost Dutchman Museum shirt. She'd had it made a few months ago when her father ordered more uniform shirts for the Lost Dutchman Ranch. She'd ordered three extra for the volunteers who would start in a few months.

Donovan stepped down from his truck and squinted in the sun before moving her way.

She met him at the door. "Festivities in town over?"

"No, but they're winding down. I watched your

dad driving the tractor with the hay wagon down Main Street. Timmy was with him."

"Dad loves the tractor and Timmy loves my dad."

A shadow crossed his face. She looked up to see if there were clouds, but not a one.

"I have a free afternoon, so I came to see your museum."

"It's not exactly mine."

"That's not what I hear." His smile was indulgent, his eyes kind.

"Don't go all sweet on me," she cautioned. "I'm still charging you admittance. That will be five dollars."

He pulled a leather wallet from his back pocket and paid. "I take it I get a private tour."

"Until our next visitor arrives."

"Which won't be until after the library event ends?"

The odds of any townies making their way to the museum were slim to none. The adults had already seen the displays. The children would be on a sugar high from the library function, and a museum wasn't a place to work off energy.

"Maybe." She started for the door to the main room but paused to let him finish reading a plaque about the museum's beginning as well as two framed newspaper articles highlighting special events, both orchestrated by her.

"Last year you had a Civil War reenactment?" He sounded surprised. "I guess I've never really connected Arizona with that time period."

"Briefly, very briefly during our territorial days, we were Confederate. Not my area of history, and I've nothing in the museum from that period. But, I have a friend who's on the Arizona Civil War Council. He convinced his group to do a performance here. We had a flag raising and the reenactment, but what brought the most guests was the period weaponry. We had live demonstrations. I even got to fire a Colt revolving rifle."

He let out a low whistle.

"But I preferred the saber."

He whistled again, leaving the framed articles and coming to stand way too close to her.

The air conditioner kicked on and Emily felt the tiniest of goose bumps prickle her arms. Good thing she could blame the air-conditioning.

"This area is all part of the Pearl Ranch. Used to be a huge operation. I don't even know the Pearl who owns it now. This tiny section was given to the city of Apache Creek a long time ago by a woman named Mary Pearl. She owned a lot of what we have on display in the gem and mineral room. I think she just wanted the world to see her collection. She died before I took over as curator."

"How long has the museum been here?"

"Just over forty-two years."

"Did she give funds to maintain the museum?"

"She did. They ran out a long time ago, though. For the last thirty years, there's an organization called Friends of Apache Creek. They started a campaign, somehow got a more-than-decent grant and really rejuvenated the museum. It was a labor of love. In the nineties, it took off and they hired the first curator."

"Not you."

She laughed. "No, I'm the third one. First one was a New York transplant who lasted about four years. He couldn't seem to get excited about the desert landscape."

To her surprise, he really looked interested as he walked behind her and soon beside her.

"It probably didn't help that back then they had a live rattlesnake as part of the display, and the curator was expected to feed it."

Donovan shook his head at the display of teeth next to a hypodermic syringe. "I've met a dozen of these guys up close and personal out at the Baer place."

"Hiding under shrubs, huh?"

"I'm not sure they were all hiding. I made sure to keep an eye out last Monday as we walked around collecting evidence."

"True," Emily agreed. "Rattlesnakes like heat."

"Fun."

"And Arizona has more rattlesnake species than anywhere else."

"I don't think anyone told George Baer."

Emily's eyes lit up. "Why didn't I think of putting that on one of my protest flyers?"

They left the rattlesnake display, went to the Jacob Waltz exhibit and finished with the Salado.

"This room's small, lots of empty space, but I've been following a couple of private collectors and I think I might be able to really make something of this display if I can get them to loan me a few artifacts. People love to see their names, gold plated, as benefactors."

"Are the Salado and Hopi related? You're Hopi, right?"

"Half-Hopi. The Salado are ancient. The term *Hopi* came about in the sixteenth century, not ancient. Before that, we were Pueblo."

"I see."

"*Hopituh Shi-nu-mu, Hopi*, it means 'the peaceful people.'" She didn't know whether to be annoyed or laugh with him, so she simply smiled and began telling him her five-year plan.

That's when the phone rang.

"Excuse me." She hurried to the front, leaving him to admire the faded black-and-white pottery.

The phone didn't ring that often. If someone called the number listed, they first heard the hours and address. They had to wait until the end of the spiel before getting to press Zero for any other questions. Most of the people who needed her help had her cell.

That reminded her. She'd never turned on her

cell after story hour. Even as she reached for the museum's phone, she opened the cupboard where her purse was and pulled out her mobile.

Seven messages.

Donovan was more interested in the Hopi than the Salado. Probably because he was interested in one particular Hopi. Their exhibit area took up both sides of one aisle. Like the Salado, they had their tools and pottery—earth tones of brown, black, yellow and orange seemed to be the colors of choice. Also, the Hopi were mask makers, and Donovan was enthralled by the differences. Some masks boasted feathers, others horns and no two were alike. One display was of a loom—much like Eva had used this morning. Then there were the kachina dolls.

Emily was correct. Benefactors did like to see their names displayed. More than five different cases had gold-plated placards stating On Loan from the Family of Naomi Humestewa.

When Emily came around the corner, he started to ask her about the Humestewas, but the look on her face stopped him.

"What's wrong?"

"Elise just called, and I need to close for a while and go check on Karl Wilcox."

"The older gentleman who lives right before the turn to your place?"

"Yes, he's not answering his cell phone. Elise has been trying him all morning."

"Why doesn't she go check on him?"

"She's alone at the ranch and apparently it's been one thing after another, including a pipe breaking in one of the cabins."

"I hope it's not the one your dad is giving me."

"What?"

"Ah, you didn't know."

She shook her head and turned for the door. "Everyone else is still at the library event. I really need to check on Karl. He fell a few weeks ago. He's pretty special to our family. Last year, he befriended Cooper's little brother at a time when Garrett needed a friend. The fall scared us more than it scared him, and that's worrisome."

"Mind if I tag along?" he asked.

To his surprise, she didn't hesitate. "If Karl's fallen, you might be a big help."

"You coming back here afterward?"

She looked at the clock. "It's already two thirty. We close at four. But this might be a simple there and back, so yes, I'll come back to work."

"Then I'll ride with you." He'd offer to drive, but some of what they'd cleaned up at the job site he'd tossed in his truck. He needn't have worried; her truck wasn't much better.

"I've been running from one place to the other," she apologized. "I keep meaning to clean."

In the front seat she had a small drill, a socket

wrench, a dark blanket—after seeing her with the skeleton, he wasn't about to ask what she used the blanket for—a fire extinguisher, two flashlights and a clipboard. A dozen pens and pencils were propped in the second cup holder.

Donovan felt strangely pleased. He could respect a woman with a front seat like this, and he'd already seen the tool chest she kept in the back.

"You've driven by Karl's." She climbed in, still needing the extra hop, and started the engine. "It's one of the oldest homes in the area, what you'd probably consider a historic ranch house circa 1933. His father built it. It's four rooms and a porch."

Circa? What kind of female said *circa*?

The kind of female he liked, he decided, answering his own question. Now that they weren't on opposing sides, she wasn't so prickly. She was soft, engaging, alluring.

And he'd be living on her daddy's ranch for a month and a half. Plus, he'd worked for the father of the last girl he'd fallen in love with. It was probably the only thing Olivia and Emily had in common.

It was enough.

The museum was on a gravel road that turned into pavement two blocks down. She drove with one hand on the wheel and gestured with the other as she talked.

"It needs some work."

"I've been wanting to see the place." His fingers itched to inspect the old walls. Even from a distance he could tell—

"I just hope Karl's all right. He's over eighty."

Donovan thought of his own father. He still lived on the dairy farm his family had owned for as long as Karl Wilcox had lived on his. Donovan was the last of his line. Right now, a neighboring farmer was renting the fields because his dad could no longer do the work.

If something happened to Raymond Russell, Donovan's dad, could his mother lift him? Could help get there in time?

"He'll be fine," Donovan said, unsure if he meant Karl or his own dad. "Tell me a bit about the house."

"It's a typical small ranch, nothing special."

He figured that meant nothing in it belonged in a museum. "Small living room?"

"Yes, one big window."

"Dining area just big enough for a table and four chairs?"

She nodded. "With floral wallpaper."

"Kitchen bigger than the dining room with linoleum floors and appliances from the 1950s?"

"Yes and no."

When he raised an eyebrow, she shared, "We've been updating the kitchen appliances for the last year because Garrett, Cooper's little brother, lives there off and on, helping around the ranch. He'll be a college freshman this coming semester. And he, uh, doesn't really cook so we needed a micro-wave, toaster and stove that worked."

Definitely a house he wanted to study. "You had to update the wiring, too?"

"Yes."

"Two bedrooms, both with room enough for beds and not much else."

"How'd you know?" she asked.

"You go back a hundred years ago, and for the most part, people were more concerned with working their land than working on their home. They built only what they needed."

There were maybe four or five houses, spread out, before they reached the end of Main Street. None of the houses added anything to the per-sonality of the area. They were all one-level dirt-brown structures, with desert landscaping. One had at least four old cars in various stages of dis-repair and a trampoline off to the side. Trash was piled on top of it.

Donovan loved Main Street. It was three blocks of businesses. What impressed him most was how a modern convenience store shared a parking lot with a restaurant clearly built in the 1950s. Right next to it was the record store where he'd recently purchased *Abbey Road* by the Beatles. It looked to be a first edition.

She turned just one block short of city lim-its and drove down another two-lane road past the high school. Once she left city limits, she apparently adhered to the belief that no speed limit posted meant no speed limit. She trailed a spiral of dust behind her and turned onto yet another two-lane road that would eventually, in just over a mile or two, lead toward her own place, the Lost Dutchman Ranch. The drive boasted only two other homes. They had personality to spare. The one closest to the Lost Dutchman Ranch was in the process of being remodeled. Donovan had already introduced himself to Jilly Greenhouse, the owner. She'd invited him to come see her middle-of-nowhere Victorian, but he'd yet to make the time.

Emily drove through the entrance of the first one, a century-old ranch house, and skidded to a stop next to an old, splotchy blue Ford.

"You can't always see the other house from the road," she said. "Up until four months ago, he had a family living there. The dad had been unemployed, and Karl wanted to help them out. We didn't worry so much then because he was never alone."

"Why'd they leave?"

"The dad got a job in Phoenix that paid more. His wife didn't think much of living this rural."

Remembering his own childhood, Donovan could understand. He'd lived his life around cows and corn. The corn had been for the cows. The cows were a 24-7 commitment. It didn't matter how close the Russells' nearest neighbor was, there was no time for visits.

Donovan never wanted a rural life again.

"The second building probably housed migrant workers at one time. I think it's a little close to the main house."

"You've been inside it?"

Emily nodded. "It's one room. Karl told me he added the bathroom back in the 1960s. His uncle was staying there at the time, and the city said he had to install it."

She headed for the front door, knocked once and opened it without waiting.

Donovan took a quick glance around. Cotton fields looked a lot different than corn, that's for sure. As much as he wanted to explore the migrant cabin, he decided to make sure Emily didn't need his help with Karl. He stepped up his pace so that he was entering into a living room on her heels. She didn't know what or whom she'd find in there. This was an out-of-the-way place. Help wasn't as close as a holler next door. The nearest house, Jilly's, was a good half mile away.

"Karl!" Emily hollered as she went room to room. He dogged her every step, amazed that she didn't hesitate before bursting into a room.

He knew about out-of-the-way places. He'd grown up on a dairy farm in Nebraska and had read *In Cold Blood* when he was sixteen. He'd spent the next six months building a tree house that he could hide in, with a rope ladder he could pull up.

"Karl wouldn't be in here," Emily said, hesitating before the last door, which he figured would lead to a second bedroom.

"Whose room is this?"

"Karl's son. He went missing…" She hesitated. "He went missing in 1979."

"Older than our skeleton."

She nodded. "Yes, and he was only seventeen when he disappeared."

Emily turned away from the room and headed to the kitchen again, exiting through a back door that banged shut behind her. Once again, he hurried to keep up.

She went to the migrant house and opened the door, peeking in and then backing out.

"Nothing?" he queried.

"Empty."

He followed her for the next fifteen minutes as she went in sheds, behind sheds and even walked a ways down a dry creek bed.

"This is actually good news," she finally said. "It means he's off with someone and just not answering his phone."

"Who does he go out with?"

"Usually Garrett, but he's in Tempe touring Arizona State University." Emily pulled out her phone and hit a button. Donovan listened as she told her sister what they'd done. She barely finished when a black Cadillac slowed at the entrance and pulled in. A moment later, Karl was exiting the passenger side, and another man exited the driver's side.

"What are you doing here?" Karl asked. "Something wrong?"

"You didn't answer your cell phone and we got worried."

Karl reached into his back pocket and pulled out a cell phone. "Hmm, how about that, turned off."

Donovan studied the Cadillac's driver. He recognized the type: slick, moneyed, used to getting what he wanted. Holding out his hand for a shake, he introduced himself. "I'm Donovan Russell."

"I'm sorry I worried you," Karl was telling Emily, who was already on the phone telling Elise that all was well.

"Randall Tucker," the driver identified himself. "I've driven by the Baer place. You're doing good work out there, quick, but no shortcuts."

"Thanks." Donovan almost said, *It will be beautiful when I finish.* But it might never be finished.

Tucker cut his glance to Emily and seemed to smirk. "I'm looking forward to seeing it." With that, he went over, patted Karl on the shoulder and said, "I'll be in touch."

After he drove away, Emily finished her phone call and asked, "Why were you with Randall Tucker?"

Karl was already at his front door, opening it,

and beckoned them to follow. "He's buying land in the neighborhood and interested in mine. I thought maybe I'd hear what he has to say."

"You want to sell?" Emily asked, incredulous.

"The man called, was interested in my place," Karl said patiently, "and I wanted to hear what he had to say."

"Randall Tucker is the man who tore down the Majestic." Emily practically spit out the words.

Donovan felt a smile form. So there was someone in Apache Creek she disliked more than him. Just figured it was someone interested in making things new instead of keeping them old.

It was the reminder Donovan needed that he and Emily weren't compatible.

Chapter Seven

❧

"What's the Majestic?" Donovan asked.

Karl filled him in while Emily phoned her other sister and dad. Donovan followed the man up the two stairs that led to the porch and then through a screen door that looked as if a good sneeze could send it flying.

"I've lived here my whole life," Karl said, switching from the Majestic to his own home. This time, Donovan had a chance to really look around the house without frantically searching for its owner. The living room was small, just enough space for a couch, an easy chair, a coffee table, a television and a fish aquarium.

"Nice," Donovan said.

Karl assumed he was talking about the fish.

"It's a twenty gallon. I couldn't keep it up until so many nosy neighbors started coming by regularly, checking up on me." He frowned at the door to the kitchen, where Emily was filling glasses with ice and water.

The frown wasn't real.

It took only a moment of Karl's explaining the landscape of the tank and types of fish for Donovan to realize he was an architect at heart and this was his creation.

"And don't forget to tell him that sometimes the fish hide," Emily said, coming back in the room and handing out water glasses.

Karl grinned. "They hide, jump out of the aquarium and triple in size. Never a dull moment. Much better than watching television."

"So, Karl." Emily's voice softened. "I still can't believe you spoke with Randall Tucker."

"Real slick fella. He said I've forty acres of prime real estate that he's willing to make an offer on."

Donovan knew of Randall Tucker. Anyone in the real estate business did. He bought old buildings, most of them in disrepair, and put up new ones. The man had a knack for figuring out the areas prime for growth. He moved in before the crowd, snatched up the best real estate for rock-bottom prices and sold at a high profit.

"And you're thinking about selling?" Emily asked softly. "Now? Why?"

"Until he called," Karl said, "I wasn't thinking of selling. In the back of my mind, I keep hoping Billy will come home. He'd be in his midfifties now. Who knows, though, maybe he's got a wife, grown kids, someone who'd want this land for what it can do."

Emily reached out a hand to touch Karl's arm, but he gently nudged it away.

Donovan didn't say anything. How could he? His father was in Mytal, Nebraska, holding on to one hundred and twenty acres, thinking someday Donovan would return home and take over.

Honor your father and your mother so that you may live long in the land your God has given you.

The look in Karl's eyes reminded Donovan that a phone call to his parents was long overdue.

Karl looked around the living room. "Truth is, I'm not wanting to sell right now. Especially not to a man who wanted to know how I'm zoned instead of how long the place has been in my family."

Emily's chin went up. Donovan could just imagine the petitions she'd do for this one.

"I'm happier than I've been for years. I've got you folks over all the time, and look at my crops. Garrett's doing a fine job. But, he's heading off for college next year, and I'm eighty-four years old. Maybe I need to be thinking about where I'll go when I can't live alone and need someone to take care of me."

To Emily's credit, she didn't argue with him.

Donovan really wanted this visit to end so he could call his parents. Karl reminded him of his dad: baseball cap, button-down shirt, jeans and tennis shoes.

"Have you looked at some of the ranches that are for sale in this area?" Emily asked. "Do you know what Jilly paid for hers?"

"Jilly's not your typical home buyer," Karl said.

"You'd be surprised," Donovan spoke up.

Both Karl and Emily looked at him.

"I've a standing offer to drop by her place," Donovan explained. "She's taken a falling-down structure and restored it and more. There are plenty of people dreaming of doing such a thing."

"Most of them don't realize the hard work it would take," Emily groused.

"That's true, but enough of them have the kind of money it takes, and it's that very thing that keeps workers like me in business."

"You're a builder not a restorer," Emily pointed out.

"Yes, but one of the jobs I'm doing next year is building a new Victorian in Florida with all the perks of the twenty-first century. I'm looking forward to it."

He was, to some degree. What he really wanted to do was build environmentally friendly homes. Not that he thought that cob was better than wood or that solar paneling was the end-all. But efficient use of what was at hand was prudent.

No, he wasn't a restorer, but he could see the potential in the four walls making up Karl Wilcox's home. He'd leave the walls of the house pretty much the way they were. Today's buyer, however, would never go for such small rooms. Donovan would utilize the berm, open up one side with windows and build belowground, Earthship style, with rounded walls. He knew right where he'd put a kiva fireplace, and he'd add flagstone floors and...

"Donovan?"

Emily interrupted his musings.

He chuckled. A belowground-level home would certainly be a hit in Apache Creek. Karl would have more company than he knew what to do with. The guests heading to the Lost Dutchman Ranch would never suspect the square feet the tiny aboveground section was hiding.

"Donovan?" Emily said again.

"You'd be surprised how many people dream of owning simpler...going back in time."

"How long does that last?" Karl wanted to know.

Donovan didn't have an answer. He dealt with new homes, usually with involved clients, who had the money to create exactly what they wanted.

"So, what did Randall offer you?"

"Five hundred thousand dollars."

Donovan didn't laugh. In the building business, tomorrow's boss might be today's competition.

"It's worth more," Emily said.

"I know, but I'm not messing with the zoning."

"Mind if I look around?" Donovan asked.

"Go right ahead." Karl finished his water and sat on the couch, studying his fish and ignoring the television.

During his first run-through of the house, Donovan had been distracted. Now, he planned to scan it more thoroughly.

Attached to the living room was a dining room with a table and four chairs. The newspaper was open to the sports page. On one side of the dining room was the kitchen. It had been built before the need for modern appliances, and counter space was at a premium. The microwave took up most of the space, followed by the coffeemaker and a canister set took up the rest. It was the stove that caught Donovan's eye. It was white enamel and looked to have four doors. Could they all be tiny ovens?

It would be hard to save this kitchen, yet it was bigger than most apartment galley kitchens.

Maybe…

He turned and went back through the dining room and found a tiny restroom, complete with a pull-cord light. On each side of the restroom were bedrooms. One had an open door. This must be Karl's.

It was mostly bed and dresser. A chair was next to the dresser and clothes were piled on it.

Donovan turned the handle of the second bedroom. It stuck a bit.

"Karl hasn't really changed Billy's room," Emily said. She stood so close behind him, he could feel her warmth.

"You've been in here, then?"

"Just once back when Garrett went missing."

"I thought his son's name was Billy."

"It was. Garrett is Elise's fiancé's little brother. The one I told you helps Karl out around the ranch. He hit a spot of trouble last year. I wasn't here so I don't know the whole story."

She pushed open the door, talking all the while, filling him in on family dynamics, something he wasn't comfortable with. His parents had been homebodies except for church, and their church had been small, just ninety members.

Billy Wilcox's room was clean, lived-in, yet not.

The posters on the wall were of Pink Floyd, Aerosmith and Led Zeppelin. School books were on a desk by the wall. They were covered in brown paper, like a grocery bag, and colored-marker words pronounced each subject: math, English, Spanish. A small television was on top of a dresser. Next to it was a typical school photo, probably Billy's senior picture. It showed a slender brown-haired youth with unruly hair and slightly protruding ears. The black T-shirt proclaimed Yes. A jean jacket was draped over the back of a chair.

"Karl never gave up hope that Billy would come home someday."

"What happened?"

"According to my sister Elise, who's become an expert on the story, Billy went off to school one morning, as usual. Karl said there wasn't anything different about the day, about his son's behavior. When it was time for him to return home, he didn't. Karl gave him some time. They'd been having struggles, the usual stuff. Billy couldn't wait to get away from Apache Creek. Karl wanted him to study, go to college, be respectful, take over.

"When it got to be six," Emily continued, "Karl called the school. No one answered, so Karl called the principal. Only then did Karl discover that Billy hadn't shown up for school at all."

"He'd run away."

"Yes, and Karl had a hard time convincing law officials to help search. Billy was two days away from eighteen, making him almost an adult. In the end, one of my uncles found a T-shirt. That's all."

Donovan picked up a Rubik's cube. It felt different than the one he'd tried in college, firmer somehow. He took a deep breath, trying not to feel Billy's frustration all those years ago. He knew; he understood. It wasn't easy to have a parent's dream rest on your shoulders, especially if you were the only son, the only one who could keep the dream alive.

Like Billy, he'd run away. He hadn't severed the relationship, though, just fractured it.

* * *

Emily stood on the porch behind the restaurant and watched the sun set. Her dad and Karl were at a table talking about old times, and Elise was at the front desk checking in a family.

Donovan's camper was parked next to the barn. She couldn't see it, but she knew it was there.

"You going to stand out here all night or take care of the couple who just sat themselves?" asked David Cook, aptly named as he was the restaurant's only cook.

Emily wanted to stay here and stare at the hazy, muted-orange sun. She didn't want to head back inside, to the smell of barbecue and corn and homemade potato chips. Usually, those were the scents of comfort and safety.

Tonight, she felt displaced, as if she wanted to be somewhere else.

With someone else.

"I'll go wait on them."

"I gave them water."

Really? Slightly stooped, more than chubby, with dark tuffs of hair on either side of his head and a swatch of baldness across the top, Cook rarely ventured from the kitchen unless it was to help restock the buffet.

"Thanks."

"Oh, and Mr. Donovan is sitting with dad and Karl."

"What?"

"I think he came in the front."

No way, no way could she have missed him loping up the path. Unless he'd not been in his cabin when she first came out here.

"I'll get him a water," Cook said, watching her. "I need a closer look."

Emily started to protest, but that would only make Cook more determined. Never, in all Emily's twenty-eight years, had Cook attempted matchmaking. But that seemed to be his intention.

As Cook walked away, Emily noticed that dark tuffs of hair were now graying and the bald spot spreading. She'd never noticed before because she was usually looking at his smiling face.

Cook had always been Emily's close friend. She, more than her sisters, liked being in the kitchen with him. Eva hadn't mastered dicing potatoes until three years ago. But she, at least, had tried. Elise, who'd never battled her weight, could live with just a microwave. Emily loved the kitchen, the smells, the laughter. Her father probably would have spit out his coffee if he knew the stories Cook, who'd traveled the rodeo circuit with him, shared with her.

Emily really needed to help out in the kitchen more often. She needed more Cook time.

Right now, what Emily really needed was more Donovan time. Adjusting the apron, she headed back into the main dining hall—one big room with lots of round tables and a buffet counter—

and headed for the couple who'd wandered in. They turned out to be tourists who'd stopped for the night and had heard about the Lost Dutchman Ranch.

"Wish we'd have known about this place earlier," the wife confided. "We'd have stayed here instead of the motel by the highway."

Her husband raised an eyebrow. He probably figured their cabins cost a lot more than the motel. That was true in the winter, when they were booked solid as people flocked to Apache Creek to enjoy the near-perfect temperatures. In summer, however, a savvy traveler could negotiate the price, grab a special.

She took their drink order and pointed out the options. Then, they helped themselves to the buffet.

Looking over at her dad's table, she noted that Cook had joined the group. What a crew. Her dad sipped iced tea and leaned forward, listening to something Karl was saying. Next to Karl, Donovan was shaking his head. Not a good sign. Jesse Campbell, Eva's husband, was bent forward, too. Hmm. Elise's fiancé, Cooper Smith, was interrupting Karl, and often.

Emily approached the table. "Hi, fellas," she interjected. "You need anything?"

Their conversation died and guilty or worried expressions swung her way.

"I'm good," Jesse said.

Everyone except Donovan agreed to more tea. Donovan stood to help himself to the buffet. Emily almost started a ticket and stopped. She hadn't been part of the agreement he and her father had reached, but if he were employed by Jacob Hubrecht, his meals would be comped.

She followed him as he filled his plate. "All moved in?"

"I'm in the last cabin in Boomtown."

"That's the biggest one."

"So your father said. I'd have gladly stayed in the Tenderfoot."

Emily shook her head. "Too much like a motel."

"I've lived in motels and my camper plenty of times. Doesn't bother me."

"Sounds lonely."

"It's an adventure," he assured her.

She'd lived in campers and motels, too, during her graduate studies as she worked on restoring ancient burial grounds in South Dakota and while building new housing on other reservations. She'd never been alone, though. There'd been other students, instructors, volunteers, construction workers and more. She'd enjoyed the camaraderie, the sense of a team on a mission.

"You hire a new crew for every house you build?" she queried.

"Usually it changes by state. Baer will arrange for a crew when I go to California next month. After that, I'll be in Florida building a few homes all in the same area. I'll keep the same crew there unless something doesn't work out."

He turned and snagged a hamburger bun before dipping a spoonful of barbecue sauce onto his plate. He followed that with a stack of homemade potato chips. He seemed to know what he was doing, already looking at-home.

She snagged a brand-new ketchup bottle to put on the plate, even though a bottle already sat in the middle of the table, then leaned against her father's chair.

"Elise has a lawyer she wants you to meet," Cooper said. "She'll arrange a meeting next week."

"Don't need one."

Emily felt a soft wave of panic. Sometimes she almost forgot that in the midst of all this, her father had been questioned by the police and a skeleton awaited identification.

"You need a lawyer, Dad," she insisted.

He smiled at her, the way he'd smiled a million times to quiet fears and let her know who was in charge.

"I have the best lawyer there is. He's told me not to worry."

For a moment, she thought he'd reach out to tussle the top of her hair, something he'd done since she was little. As the shortest of the three sisters, she'd often had to assert herself so they didn't take advantage, or worse—try to take care of her, do things for her.

Forcing her gaze away from her father's, she looked out one of the big panoramic windows toward the Superstition Mountains. A faint thread of clouds hovered above one peak. The Pima Indians believed the mountain to be a guardian, watching over the land below. She managed a half smile. The mountain would be the ultimate silent witness. Not good enough.

"Justice usually prevails," Donovan agreed.

"You really believe that?" Emily's words were a bit sharper than she meant them to be. But then, it wasn't his dad whose initials were on a knife that might have been used in a homicide. Thank goodness the original receipt said only one knife had been engraved for him.

"I do," Donovan said, "and I'm surprised you don't. Your father bowed his head in prayer before the meal we ate last Friday. He didn't seem a bit worried when I left. And didn't he pray that they'd identify the bones quickly so the family could be notified?"

"It would be awful not knowing," Emily agreed. "He does believe the same as you. And yesterday at church, Sam Miller said we have at least ten men in Apache Creek with the initials J.H."

"How many women?" Donovan asked.

"What?"

"How many women have those initials? Then, too, you'd have to look at both maiden and married names."

He surprised her. "Historically, poison is the female weapon of choice," she finally responded. "In the middle of nowhere, it's hard to imagine a female overpowering a male with a knife the size we found."

"Hard to imagine, but not impossible."

Cooper stood. "I need to get home. Garrett's got some papers I need to look at. I can't believe he's decided to head off to university and major in agricultural studies."

"You going to your house or mine?" Karl asked.

"Mine."

"Well, you might want to call. When I left to come over here, he was in my field. Something about cotton and nitrogen management."

Donovan laughed and said, "My mind stops at one for the mouse, one for the crow, one to rot and one to grow."

"I've heard that one," Jacob said. "Where did you hear it?"

"Growing up, from my dad."

Donovan was the only one still eating. The others stood, but Emily's father got waylaid before he made it to the door. Jilly Greenhouse, their nearest neighbor, and one who did not like to cook, wooed him to her table.

"A little romance there?" Donovan asked.

"No, she just likes knowing what's going on." Watching her dad and Jilly now, Emily rethought her response. Since the discovery of the skeletal remains and knife, Jilly had been here every evening.

Could she be giving advice to Emily's father, too?

"Neighborly," Donovan said. "I might really enjoy working here. I've already started drawing a mock-up of what the buildings could look like."

"Timmy has to name it something besides Tinytown," Emily said. "It doesn't go with the Lost Dutchman's personality."

"Your dad mentioned something about Timmy coming up with the name. It is the kind of name kids will go for."

Donovan took hold of her elbow, tugging her down into the chair next to him. His grip was strong, firm, and she felt it all the way to her knees.

Not possible.

"I'll tell Timmy to let you name the movie theater. Or, maybe I'll build a tiny museum. Would that make you happy?"

"It might," she sniffed, staying in the chair for only a moment. She knew she had customers looking around for her. It was time to focus on the present, not the past or the future.

"I like your future brother-in-law."

"Cooper's easy to like."

"I enjoyed hearing about Cooper's horse, too."

Uh-oh. Emily had a feeling she knew where

this was going. "You heard all about Percy Jackson, then?"

"I did. And Cooper said something about a different horse named Harry Potter."

Emily couldn't help but smile. "Did he tell you I named Pinocchio, Snow White and Cinderella?"

"Yes, and he told me that Cinderella has focus issues."

"My dad wouldn't hurt anyone," Emily said suddenly, needing to get the words out. "He—he won't even put a horse down until there's no other choice. We've about five horses that are too old to ride. Dad lets them retire."

"You don't have to convince me," Donovan said. "I just wish the body had turned up someplace besides my job site."

Emily bit her lip. He'd just reminded her of his priorities. She'd needed to hear that because she'd been starting to trust him. Better to keep him at arm's length.

"Yes, there is that." Leaving him to eat, she hurried and did one last sweep of the room, refilling teas, restocking sugar bowls and cleaning up a ketchup spill.

Timmy helped with cleaning tables, knowing it would earn him an extra hour of video-game playing as well as keep his parents happy.

Taking a bus tub into the kitchen, she set it on the conveyor belt by the dishwasher and asked,

"Cook, what were you guys talking about? You looked so serious."

"He's a good guy," Cook responded. "But he's not one who will stay. And I can't see you leaving here."

"He's just another guy. I'm not leaving here, and you didn't answer the question."

"We were discussing Karl's land, how much it's worth, how it's zoned and why the sudden interest."

"What did you decide?"

"Mostly that it's Karl's to do with what he wants. He thinks if he can change his zoning designation from agricultural to residential, he can get more than Tucker offered."

The air swished out of Emily's lungs.

Karl couldn't sell.

"Whose idea was that?"

"Donovan brought it up, but your father and Jesse would have if Donovan hadn't."

"Why now?"

"Your father thinks that Randall Tucker made good money when he bought the Majestic for a song and put up the apartment building. He's wanting to do it again."

Emily grabbed a rag from the sink, turned on the hot water and headed for the door. She almost missed Cook's next words.

"Then, too, your father thinks that when the Baer house went up, showing that there were buyers for luxury homes in this area, Tucker got a whole new idea."

"Because of the Baer house?" she whispered, picturing how Donovan looked sitting in the rustic dining room of the Lost Dutchman Ranch, remembering his arm on her elbow pulling her down beside him.

"The Baer house does come with a view from every side." Cook quoted an article from the newspaper. Emily remembered who'd made the statement.

Donovan.

In a roundabout way, Donovan was responsible for Tucker pursuing Karl.

She wished again that Baer had never heard of Apache Creek.

Then Emily wouldn't be torn over her feelings for one Donovan Russell.

Chapter Eight

After leaving the restaurant, Donovan walked to his cabin. There, he hesitated, rethinking the contract he'd just signed. Jacob didn't need him. Not if the man had designed this cabin.

Donovan could live here.

Boomtown was the farthest away from the main house, giving it a seclusion that Rawhide and Tenderfoot didn't have. In case a guest didn't want a three-to-five-minute walk, all he had to do was call the phone desk and he'd be picked up by either a golf cart or quad—the guest got to choose.

Donovan didn't mind walking.

The five cabins formed a half circle but each had about a quarter acre of land. Even as last minute as his arrival had been, a Welcome Donovan placard had been placed by the front door. Donovan didn't open the door; instead, he sat in one of the rocking chairs on the porch and just enjoyed the view.

Jacob had not crowded his dude ranch. He'd spread the buildings out, making sure that guests would note the mountains first, then the horses and main structure, and finally the other guest lodgings.

Donovan could have been happy here. Sure, he could see that Jacob's daughters had pitched in, earned their keep, but they'd had fun and free time, too.

He'd seen the photos of Eva at state fairs exhibiting her weavings, of Elise competing in rodeo events and of Emily onstage in school plays, all dressed up.

In the distance he heard a coyote, then another, until a full chorus was echoing. Something orangey was in the air, but he couldn't identify it, and it had been a long time since he stopped and smelled the roses. He was pretty sure the scent wasn't the same from his camper.

He pushed himself to his feet. Melancholy he did not need. Plus, if he sat out here any longer he might start imagining what it would feel like should one Emily Hubrecht be sitting next to him, talking about the sites, her day and asking him about his.

The only people who asked about his day were his employer and his employees.

Come to think of it, Olivia hadn't really asked him about his day unless she was worried it would interfere with the plans she'd made. And her daddy would always let Donovan off early if it made his daughter happy.

Walking past the knotty pine and to the door, he unlocked it and stepped inside.

The cabin's interior was even better. A giant window spread across the front. Two more were in the kitchen. Donovan had two bedrooms, one on each end, and the living/dining room was light wood, open and not heavy on unnecessary furniture, except for the old-fashioned bathtub in the middle of the room.

He figured there was some story about the bathtub.

He set his keys on the table and headed for the shower. It had been a long but interesting day.

He'd no more than dried off and settled in front of the television to channel surf when his phone sounded. He checked the number, not one he recognized, and swiped the phone on before saying hello.

Ten minutes later, Donovan ended the call. No longer in the mood for television, he headed into the master bedroom to sleep. Maybe if he read for a while, he could get past the concern he was feeling.

When Baer had simply walked away from the build, Donovan figured he could no longer be surprised by the twists and turns of the construction business.

He was wrong.

* * *

Sunday-morning breakfast was pretty much self-serve. Emily took two pancakes from the steamer, added bacon and eggs to her plate, and sat down. Timmy brought her milk and took a seat next to her. He bowed his head in prayer, saying, "God, thank You for this food, for this ranch and for everything else, especially Legos. Please be with Eva. Amen."

"What's wrong with Eva?" Emily asked.

"She's not going to church with us today."

"She's not feeling good?"

"She walked all night. I tried to stay up with her, but she didn't really go anywhere except from the living room to the bathroom to the kitchen. I fell asleep on the couch."

Walking wasn't the way Eva usually dealt with issues. If something bothered her, she usually worked her loom. But she'd spent hours weaving at the library event; maybe she was loomed out.

"I slept on that couch many a night," Emily shared.

"Daddy might stay home with her."

"Okay," Emily allowed, "now we're getting serious."

"He said I could go to church with you and Grandpa."

"Sounds good."

"You think Donovan will start on Tinytown today?"

"No, I think today is Sunday and Grandpa will want Donovan to get started tomorrow."

"We play on Sunday."

"So we do," she agreed. "But Sunday, for many, is a day of rest. Don't worry. Donovan's right here. He'll get Tinytown going in no time."

"I wonder if Grandpa would let Donovan build a penny arcade. Wouldn't that be cool?"

"Where did you hear about penny arcades?"

"Taylor Hamm came back from Colorado talking about one that he went to, near a place called Pikes Peak. It sounds like a fun place."

Emily tousled the top of Timmy's head. Sometimes she forgot that he'd spent the early years of his life not doing much, rarely going to parks or museums or swimming pools. His mother had been battling drug addiction, and his father—Jesse—hadn't known about Timmy's existence.

The ranch, to Timmy, was Oz. But, he'd never traveled much, not to the Grand Canyon or to the beach or anywhere.

"Someday your parents will take you there. I promise."

"Might be even better to bring it here," Timmy said, much too seriously.

"Bring what here?"

Emily recognized the deep voice and was suddenly glad she was already dressed for church. Looking at Donovan, she noted the perusal he gave her. He'd seen her in work clothes—dark shirts and khakis—and yesterday he'd seen her in Native attire.

Both her sisters dressed Western no matter what, with Eva preferring turquoise, belts and fringe. Elise was a no-fuss kind of woman. Emily, though, loved to dress up—frilly and whirls.

Definitely worth it. She'd impressed him, and all it took was a dark red knit maxi dress with a high halter, cutout neckline and nipped waist. The skirt flowed around her legs, so that if she twirled, it might flare as far as the table she sat at.

Gold sandals complemented the gold bracelets on her wrists, the dangling gold earrings, and the gold and crystal hair comb that stretched from her right ear to the top of her forehead. She'd let her black hair hang loose.

"You look nice," Donovan said.

"I always try to look my best for God."

He blinked.

"Me, too," Timmy piped up. He was wearing a white shirt and black pants. Well-worn tennis shoes finished his outfit, and she remembered Eva lamenting that Timmy seemed to grow a shoe size a week.

"Your dad around?"

"He's down with the horses."

For a moment, she thought Donovan would

leave to go join her father. Instead, he took a plate, filled it and sat down beside her.

She'd cleaned her plate while talking with Timmy, meaning she'd get to do most of the talking.

"There's plenty of time. If you want, you can come to church with us. It's just Dad, Timmy and me. Eva doesn't feel good, so she and Jesse are staying home."

"What about your other sister?"

"Elise and her fiancé are in Two Mules."

"Two Mules?"

"It's a town a few hours from here. Elise works with teenagers and horses. She has two kids going to a rodeo next month, and she wanted extra time with them."

"There's really a town named Two Mules?" Donovan shook his head.

"It's pretty small."

"Smaller than Apache Creek?"

"What? You don't like small?"

He hesitated before sharing, "I grew up in a very small town in Nebraska. It was over an hour's bus ride just to get to school."

"Cool," Timmy said.

"Not when you had to get up at four in the morning to help with the cows, and then get dressed, eat breakfast and get to the bus stop by six in the morning. By the time the school bell rang, I'd been up four hours."

"You were raised on a dairy farm?" Emily asked. She'd researched him when he moved here to build the Baer home, and then again when her dad starting talking about hiring him. She'd known he was from Nebraska, but she hadn't realized how rural or that he'd been raised on a dairy farm.

"I was."

"That's surprising."

He raised an eyebrow and smiled. "Because I'm so debonair now?"

"What's *debonair*?" Timmy queried.

"It means he thinks he belongs on the cover of a men's fashion magazine or starring as James Bond."

"Who's James Bond?"

Emily held up a hand. She knew how long this game could go on. To Donovan, she said, "I can't think of many jobs harder than dairy farming. It's 24-7 with no holidays."

"You pretty much summed it up. Add to that we lived in the middle of nowhere. There were three families within easy driving distance. None of them had kids my age."

"You didn't like living on the farm."

"I didn't like it, and I went off to college and never turned back."

"When I was in college," Emily shared, "I traveled as far as South Dakota in order to complete my graduate studies. I enjoyed every minute, but

I had to come home to visit at least every three or four months because I missed my family."

"I don't make it home much. I've been busy building a career. My family understands."

She couldn't argue with the busy part. She'd found a whole list of projects during her search, some started while he was a freshman in college. He'd been part of a group that helped rebuild a small village in Mexico after a tornado destroyed most of it.

Just a few months ago, she'd thought this the only thing they had in common.

After college, he'd worked for a firm that built homes in the Omaha and Council Bluffs, Iowa, area. They weren't quite luxury homes, but they were close. They were upscale suburbia.

And they didn't compare at all to the Lost Dutchman Ranch.

"How long has it been since you've been home?"

He hesitated, and Emily could almost imagine him counting his fingers. "Three years."

Three years! She'd wilt if she were separated from Apache Creek for that long. She'd die if she were separated from her family.

"And that wasn't really home. I met my parents in York, Nebraska, at a restaurant about an hour's drive for them. I wanted them to meet my fiancée."

"Elise is a fiancée," Timmy put in. Emily had to admire how he'd been trying to keep up with the conversation. "It means you'll be getting married."

"You've been in Apache Creek for months. Why hasn't your fiancée come to visit?" Emily tried to sound interested, very afraid her voice would sound creaky.

What was wrong with her? She had no hold on Donovan Russell. She'd only been on friendly terms with him for a week, ever since he'd gotten the "step down" order from Tate Luxury Homes. She'd been a bit more impressed when he'd helped her comb the Baer land looking for evidence. He'd even had John Westerfield help out.

Then, there'd been yesterday.

It had been a long time since she'd liked someone from the male species.

Too long.

"Olivia and I broke up quite a while ago. We—" he hesitated "—we weren't good together. Very different."

"You liked her well enough to introduce her to your parents."

"It was the right thing to do. I'd proposed, she had a ring and we were planning a future. My parents needed to meet her."

"But you didn't take her home? Why not?"

One side of his mouth lifted in a half smirk. "Olivia Tate on a dairy farm. Not happening."

"Tate," Emily said slowly. "As in Tate Luxury Homes."

"You got it."

"I'd go visit a dairy farm in a heartbeat." Emily

noticed something in his eyes, a faraway look. She didn't know if he was thinking of Olivia or his youth. She hoped it was his youth. "What was the best thing about it? There has to be something."

"One summer my dad and I built a tree house. It lasted maybe a year before it fell apart, and Dad didn't have time to build another one. I tried by myself, but I think my idea of what the completed project should look like far exceeded both my skill level and the tree's perimeter."

"I'd love a tree house," Timmy said.

"How long," Emily asked, almost in a whisper, "since you've been home and stared at the tree where you tried to build a tree house?"

Donovan didn't answer. Instead, he finished the last bite of pancake and Emily's dad walked into the restaurant, checking his watch for the time and giving Timmy a nod that they needed to hurry.

"We'll wait for you if you want to come to church with us." She really hoped he'd attend.

"No, I've got some things to do today."

"You could build me a tree house," Timmy said. "That would be a good thing to do today."

"Probably not today." The faraway look was back in his eyes, but Emily saw a hint of the boy he'd been.

"We need to get going," her father hollered across the room.

"Coming, Grandpa," Timmy said.

Emily stood, starting to gather up their dishes,

but Donovan put a hand over hers. It was warm, strong, with long, calloused fingers. "I'll take care of this. You look much too nice to risk spilling something."

Like the half-full glass of milk Timmy had walked away from.

She thought she heard him say something as he headed toward the dish window. She thought she heard him say, "Twelve years."

Twelve years!

Why?

The Miner's Lamp, a more or less rustic café, was the second building on Main Street. At eleven, it was fairly empty: too late for breakfast, too early for the church crowd. Donovan took a big corner booth, checked the time on his cell phone and then went to messages.

He had none. Reading his old messages, he realized that 100 percent of his conversations were work related. Not a real friend in the bunch. That was part of being a traveling man.

"Here you are. I've been running a bit late all day."

Randall Tucker, Donovan knew, was in his sixties, called New York home—although he rarely stayed there—and had been born and bred in the real estate world.

Randall easily slid into the booth, placing his briefcase beside him.

Last night, after talking with the man, Donovan did his homework and looked at the Tucker Organization website. At first glance, the real estate portion of Tucker's company wasn't obvious. Randall's father, Rudy Tucker, had started the business. Rudy seemed more inclined to promote his political moves, television appearances and self-help book than the business that had made him a multimillionaire.

Randall had two older brothers. They looked to be following in their father's footsteps: aggressive, shrewd and rebounding well.

Randall was a bit of a black sheep, not in behavior, but in business leanings. For the past twenty-odd years, he'd been in the business of tearing down the old and putting up the new and always in small towns. There was an odd four-year gap, just a few years ago, where he'd simply lived in San Diego and apparently backed away from the real estate business.

"Just got here myself," Donovan said, noting that the man hadn't said sorry.

The waitress, Jane de la Rosa, placed water and menus in front of them and walked off without asking if they were ready. The faintest pursing of her lips told Donovan that she disapproved of their meeting.

No doubt she'd be texting Emily.

A friend, not a business acquaintance.

"Glad you could meet me," Randall said. "I

went out to the Baer place yesterday and walked around. I'm surprised you weren't at work. It's been cleared, what with the body and all."

Donovan didn't know if Randall was fishing, clueless or already knew that Baer no longer wanted to live in Apache Creek. "Things are a bit up in the air right now."

Randall didn't even pause. "I ate at the Lost Dutchman Ranch earlier in the week. Jacob showed me the plans you drew up for Tinytown. Impressive."

"It will be a nice change. I like being creative."

"Karl told me you thought his place would be perfect for a belowground-level home."

"I shared with him a gut reaction when he mentioned that he might sell. I'd have to do some preliminary studies to see if such a structure would really work there."

"It would work." Randall raised his hand, beckoning Jane over. Quickly he ordered, and then looked at Donovan, clearly expecting the same.

"I'll just have iced tea," Donovan told Jane. Then, he mused, "It probably would work, but would it sell, be low maintenance, increase in value?"

"Not in the current economy and locale."

"What's the occupancy ratio of your apartment building?" Donovan asked.

"Forty percent. Apache Creek is a slow-growth area, and I'm confident that in the next two years we'll go to a hundred percent. Plus, this isn't a migrant area. People who move in will stay. There won't be a high turnover."

"You make money from high turnover," Donovan pointed out.

"Only if there's someone next in line to rent."

Jane came and put drinks in front of the men.

"You didn't call me to talk apartments," Donovan said. "Why did you call me?"

"I'm in the process of buying land for a development. I have my own people, but, quite frankly, I think if I'd made the apartment complex match the historic feel of Apache Creek, I'd have sixty percent occupancy. I can gloat over projections, but I'm used to a quicker return for my investment."

"And?"

"I know George Baer personally."

That answered one question. Randall wasn't fishing or clueless. He knew about the radon gas and why Baer had halted construction.

"I've been in both his other homes."

Donovan had, too. They were lavish, ridiculous and seldom occupied. *Sterile* was the word that came to mind.

"I could tell," Randall continued, "how you influenced his choices of open space and options. The other two homes, the builder gave George whatever he asked for. You, however, managed to convince him that quality is better than quantity."

Since the Baer home was fifteen thousand square feet, quantity was a given and quality secondary.

"I thought about making Baer an offer," Tucker said, "but the radon gas made the newspaper. It will be a while before the stigma disappears. Never mind that every house has radon gas."

Donovan hated to think of the Baer home being a half-finished monument, a pimple on the skin of...

Whoa, he was starting to think like Emily.

"I've sent George Baer some ideas on how to bring the levels down," Donovan shared. "He's not answered yet."

"If I know Baer," Tucker said, "he'll move on to bigger and better things. In this case, not better— you built a beautiful home—but he'll go bigger."

Emily would be happy about this news.

"Here's the thing," Tucker continued. "I've got plans for this little town. The place is ripe for a subdivision or two, reasonably priced of course."

Donovan looked out the restaurant's window. For the most part, this section of Apache Creek was dirt colored. The Main Street hosted a convenience store, bar and grill, fast food restaurant, an auto repair shop, and a park. A lone tumbleweed crossed the road, a time traveler from a distant era.

"Even for Arizona, this town's Western. I don't see a growth spurt in its future. For one thing, no jobs, and for anoth—"

"I'm not really thinking of families. I'm thinking more of retirees. If you look across this portion of Arizona, we've got lots of retirement communities. There's Sun City, Scottsdale, Prescott."

"All have a cost of living much higher than here."

"My point exactly. If you look at where people are planning to retire present day, you'll see Yuma, Nogales, places much like Apache Creek."

"You do see the big picture," Donovan admitted, pausing as Jane set breakfast in front of Tucker. Now that he thought about it, Tucker's plan made perfect sense. "But, why are you telling me? I work for Tate Luxury Homes, and I'm not planning on quitting anytime soon."

"Not for two years."

Donovan finished his tea in one long gulp. "I take it you know Nolan Tate, too."

"His father and mine are friends. I can't say that I'm overly fond of him."

"He's my employer, and I have a few contracts to finish before I can even think about a career move."

Tucker nodded and took a few bites of his biscuits and gravy. Then, he said, "I'd like to pay off your debt to him, put you in my employ and let you design my masterpiece. I'll give you plenty of say. I like the originality you put into the homes you built in Cannes, Nebraska."

It had been a long time since Donovan thought

about Cannes. He'd designed three blocks of homes, all virtually the same size and all different. The town's critics didn't appreciate how just one neighborhood didn't fit into the cookie-cutter mold. The people who purchased the homes loved that they wouldn't accidentally pull into the wrong driveway at ten at night because every house looked the same.

"Masterpiece, huh?"

Emily, Donovan knew, wouldn't call it a masterpiece. She'd called it a monstrosity.

"Let me show you," Tucker said. He opened his briefcase, took out some blueprints and soon Donovan was looking at the type of development that was a dime a dozen in almost every city.

"Tract housing," Donovan noted.

"It's easy, it's affordable, it's quick," Randall shot back.

"Like your apartment building with forty percent occupancy."

"See," Randall said, "that's why I'm talking to you. I think, together, we can come up with something that will do this town good."

"I don't do the Levittown concept."

"And, if we can come up with a plan, I'd like to stay away from that concept myself. Think about it. Quite honestly, somewhere in this town, I'll establish a housing development. With or without you. If you sign on, I promise I'll listen to your design ideas."

"So, instead of being in debt to Nolan Tate, I'd be in debt to you." Donovan didn't phrase it as a question but as a statement.

"Difference being, I like your style. I might even hire you to build me a tree house. Also, someday I'll be wanting a partner and I guarantee, I'll not go bankrupt. If that was going to happen, it would have happened by now. Also, I'll garnish your wages for repayment, but when you've paid off the debt, if you're not happy, you can walk away knowing that the places you built had your stamp on them and that it wasn't just the wealthy who could afford them. Difference being, you won't have to constantly deal with an angry almost father-in-law."

Donovan wanted to say *better the enemy you know than the enemy you don't,* but held his tongue. He'd gotten further in this business than some of his peers by not reacting rashly. "Let me think about it."

Chapter Nine

Monday morning, no need for an alarm clock, Donovan rolled out of bed bright and early. Some habits were hard to break. Five was way too early for breakfast but perfect for soul-searching. He dressed in jeans and a T-shirt, grabbed the thriller he'd started a good month ago, and headed outside to sit on the porch in the early hour. A somewhat cool breeze greeted him, bending a few limbs and rippling the grass. From what he'd heard from his crew and now the Hubrechts, in a few weeks the cool would cease to be.

The rocking chair creaked under his weight as he pushed it close to the porch railing so he could put his feet up. Setting his book on the ground, he turned on his phone and checked his emails. Nothing from Nolan Tate. If the man wanted, he'd have Donovan clocking in. There wasn't a crew that couldn't use a good worker. This was just a way to prolong the agony and let Donovan know who had the power. Didn't matter. Donovan was doing the right thing, paying off his debt, being the bigger man. There was nothing from Randall Tucker, either. No surprise. Donovan figured the man would wait until Donovan came to him. And how he wanted to. Imagine severing his connection to Nolan Tate, not having a constant reminder of Olivia and having a little more say in what he was doing. Tucker was correct. Apache Creek would be an awesome place to retire. The Superstition Mountains alone were worth the move. Add to that the Lost Dutchman Ranch, the museum and the sixty-year-old library… And a five-foot-nothing dark-haired beauty who'd hate him forever if he built a tract of residential homes right next door to her.

Donovan shook his head. He was getting soft. He'd only been on her good side for less than a week, so keeping on her good side shouldn't be an incentive. She was buried all the way to her knees in Apache Creek's soil. He was more a shake-the-dust-from-the-bottom-of-his-feet kind of guy. As much as she spouted the Word, he doubted she'd appreciate the comparison. Come to think of it, he didn't appreciate the comparison. If he was shaking the dust from his feet, it meant he found the place, the Lost Dutchman Ranch, unworthy, lacking, doomed. He remembered more of his childhood Sunday school than he'd thought. His parents couldn't get him home from after-school baseball practice or to games, so he didn't get to play. But every Sunday morning—except for life-or-death matters—they were at church.

Donovan shifted his focus back to the phone. Three emails waited for him. One was from an electrician he'd worked with a year ago. The man wanted a job. Donovan responded with a *sorry* and *if anything comes up, I'll let you know*. Another was from a man looking for someone to build a tree house for his son. Donovan emailed that he was booked for two years but could recommend another builder. The last was from Olivia. It had been over a month since her last text. He opened her missive and studied the photo of her posed on a beach in Aruba. A man stood beside her. The sun was behind them, the waves curving.

Olivia didn't include text. Her message was clear: *here's what you're missing*. Smiling, hoping the ground didn't open up and swallow him, Donovan bowed his head. *Thank You, Father. Thank You for bringing me to this place, letting me see what I was missing and putting me back in the company of sane people. Amen.*

Immediately after saying amen, he wondered just how long those sane people would remain his friends should he take Tucker up on his offer.

Distant laughter echoed. A horse whinnied and then came laughter. Picking up his book, Donovan headed back inside the cabin and looked at the Lost Dutchman Ranch notebook on his dresser.

There was a morning ride, supposedly leaving at five thirty. Judging by the laughter, it was still in the prep stage. All he really needed were his socks and shoes, which he quickly tugged on before heading back outside. When he rounded the corner of the barn, Jacob was starting down the trail with seven people following him. Emily was number seven.

"Got room for one more?" he shouted.

She reined her horse, nodding to her father, and turned back to him.

"You know how to ride?"

"Do you know how to tell a story?"

She smiled, still looking a bit sleepy eyed. This morning she wore an old DC Talk T-shirt and jeans. Her boots were brown and worn. Her hair, in a ponytail, swayed slightly as she dismounted and looked him up and down.

"Been a while?" she asked.

"Yes."

"Would you rate yourself highly experienced, average or low?"

No way did he want to rate himself average in front of Emily Hubrecht. "I'm experienced."

"Had horses on that Nebraska farm?"

"Yes."

She gave him Cinderella.

"I like her," Donovan said, stroking the brown nose all the way up to the white square on the horse's forehead. Some would call it a star, but

Donovan figured if it was a star, then it had been stepped on. "Is she the one with focus issues?"

"Don't get too relaxed," she warned him.

Together they saddled Cinderella and then both nudged their horses to a trot in order to catch up with Jacob, who was well out of sight.

"I've been wanting to ask—" Donovan angled his horse so he was next to Emily and her horse "—have the police spoken with your father any more? They've not contacted me with questions in over a week."

"Elise says that with no witness to the possible crime and no fingerprints on the knife, there's nothing that can be done."

"Your dad's probably relieved."

She looked ahead of him, at the distant curving line of horses, acting a little more withdrawn than she had yesterday. "He is. We all are. But, the skeleton belongs to somebody's son, brother, father, husband. We don't know. That means there's someone else out there who doesn't know."

"With DNA sampling, it's likely we'll have a name soon enough."

She shook her head. "Only on television. In real life, it could be years before our skeleton gets tested. Then, too, we don't know if anyone from his family has ever had their DNA taken. Often, especially with children or those who have no family members who've served in the military, you get a DNA profile, but there is no match."

She was just as good at talking dead bodies as she was telling stories about corn maidens or pointing out history in her museum.

They caught up with the other riders and easily took the rear position. Jilly Greenhouse rode ahead closer to Jacob, who was explaining, "In the winter, we take longer rides. I've gone on all-day outings that took us from the ponderosa pines to the desert and saguaro cactus. We don't do that in June."

Donovan studied the landscape. He'd gone on only a few escorted trail rides, usually with buyers who wanted to see their purchasing options. He'd never been impressed because he'd always felt that the horses, following the same dirt trail day after day, were moving in rote. The guides, too, although some were better than others.

Not so with Jacob Hubrecht. The dirt underneath the horses was a path for only the first fifteen minutes. Then, it was a mixture of grass, dirt and sand, whichever way Jacob or even one of the guests decided to go. Jacob was a natural guide, pointing out flora and fauna—juniper, piñon pine and manzanita—as well as animals. Rabbits seemed the most common but about an hour into the ride, they stumbled across three mule deer.

They came to a shady spot with a downed tree that someone had chopped so it acted more like a bench than anything else. Jacob nodded at Emily and they dismounted, helped the inexperienced riders down, and then took a break.

Jacob gave everyone bottled water, and Emily handed out fruit and crackers. Two teenagers took off exploring. Their parents did the same. Donovan figured they were really keeping their kids in sight. Jilly and the other rider stayed close to Jacob. Donovan watched as the man, who he figured was an advanced beginner when it came to sitting a horse, asked questions and wrote things down in a small spiral notebook.

"I think he's a writer," Emily shared, sitting on the log with Donovan and opening her bottled water. "We get quite a few. I guess in the romance world, cowboys are pretty popular."

Donovan might be willing to put on a cowboy hat if Emily were willing to get a little closer.

"He doesn't look like a romance writer," Donovan observed.

"No, he's probably true crime or maybe even into the whole Jacob Waltz legend."

"You get a lot of people asking about Waltz?"

"Yes, because my dad named the ranch after the legend."

They both watched for a few minutes as Emily's dad told some story with lots of hand movements and Jilly butted in every once in a while. Jacob didn't seem to mind.

Looking away from them, Emily focused on Donovan and said, "You're not a bad rider. I wasn't sure what to expect."

"I had my own horse growing up. Risky Business. I think my dad gave him to me when I was about four. I rode him almost every day until I turned sixteen."

"Then you weren't interested anymore?"

"No, I was still interested. I rode him three or four times a week, but I wanted to play baseball and go to town more often. Then, Risky developed laminitis."

"Did you put him down?"

"My father did. We didn't have extra money, and he'd been thinking about the upkeep. The horse was old when given to me. I remember my dad saying he had a good life."

She seemed to soften toward him a bit. For a moment, he thought she might reach out, touch his hand. He'd have liked that.

"Growing up on a dairy farm must have been hard."

"I can't imagine anything that requires more time and energy," he agreed. "It wasn't the life for me. Not only do I not want to be tied down, but at heart I'm a city boy."

Maybe he imagined it, but when Emily Hubrecht nodded as if understanding what he meant, she looked a little sad.

And he'd made her feel that way again.

* * *

Emily's dad was still talking. This two-hour ride might turn into three, but none of the riders seemed to care. Especially Jilly, who opened a bottled water and held it out to Jacob, making sure he drank some.

Looking at Donovan, Emily figured she might as well kill some time. She was stuck with him for about a month and a half, and then the city boy would no longer be tied down to Apache Creek.

"How did you get into building?"

"I already told you about the tree house my dad and I built, the one that fell apart."

"How old were you?"

"Probably eight or nine. I didn't build another until my third year of college. I knew then that I'd be majoring in architecture. I went home with one of my roommates. He lived on a farm, too, in Melbourne, Iowa, except his place was crops only. I got paid as a field hand, and in our spare hours, he and I built his little brother a tree house that was so much more."

She knew the details because his best friend now kept a blog. She'd actually found a copy of the newspaper article that showed the elaborate tree house.

"After that, Keith and I did two more, this time for pay, in the same small town. If I'd have been smarter, I'd have finished college and started my own small business right then. But I thought that working for someone established and building custom homes and businesses would pay more."

"Does it?" Emily asked. "Because I found a photo on the web of a tree house you built in Burlington, Iowa, just five years ago, and it looked expensive."

"It was, for a tree house, but tree houses don't take nearly as long as real houses. I'd make up the cost by sheer number of projects. Plus, I'd never get bored."

"I'm rarely bored. There's always something to do here."

"I believe you, but will you feel the same in ten years when you realize that you'll live and die where you've always lived, seldom seeing how others lived?"

"You say that like it's a bad thing."

"My dad was born and raised in the house he still lives in. He's been to Iowa and Illinois. Both times because a close relative passed away. I don't mind hard work. Matter of fact, my dad taught me its value. But, it's so much more satisfying to have fun while you're working hard."

"So, to you, building the Baer house was fun."

She felt some satisfaction when he took a moment to answer. "Many years ago, I signed on as designer and project manager for a company that built one-of-a-kind custom homes. They were up-and-coming. They hired me on because I told them I'd like to build homes that had tree houses connected to them. Within six months, I joined as a partner. It didn't mean a raise in pay. The two brothers who started the company were just a little older than me, dreamers, and they'd sunk all their money into it. I knew it was a risk, but, Emily, if it had taken off…"

It was truly the first time she'd seen him this passionate. "What was the company's name?" She'd found no mention of it online.

"Brewster and Brewster. Then, Brewster and Russell. They were trying hard to get a network interested in following one of us as we built a unique home, one meant for families to live in and enjoy."

"What happened?"

"Plain and simple, we went bankrupt. I lost everything."

Emily couldn't imagine losing everything. Part of her wasn't even sure what everything might be. Probably the worst scenario would be the Lost Dutchman Ranch, but with her father and Eva's leadership, the place was doing better than ever, even in the summer. And, really, it was a place. What made it special was the people.

Kinda like church.

She could lose her museum job. She always worried about that. Unlike Donovan, though, she'd not be heartbroken over lack of funds, because she had the ranch and her storytelling. Well, if the museum closed down, she'd be heartbroken over the loss of history, both current and what she could add in the future.

"So," she said, "how did you wind up with Tate Luxury Homes?"

"Isn't it about time to start riding again?" He stood, finishing the last of his water and looking around. Emily stood, too. The reporter was sitting, leaning against the tree and writing all by himself. Her dad and Jilly were walking together, following the path the family had taken.

Emily and Donovan were pretty much alone.

"That's one of the great things about the Lost Dutchman Ranch," Emily said. "We've schedules, but they're not so strict that they cannot be deviated from."

"You're blessed."

"If you don't want to discuss working for Tate, you don't have to. I'm just curious."

He walked back to Cinderella, a bit slowly, which gave her an opportunity to change the subject.

"It's been a while since you've ridden."

"Quite a while." He stuck the empty water bottle in the saddle pack. "I like Cinderella. Which horse are you on?"

"This is Snow White. She's a registered Arab quarter horse. I've had her since I was four."

"Which makes her?

"Old enough to know better than share her age."

Donovan half smirked. "I think you're between twenty-five and thirty."

"Thirty!"

"Aww, closer to twenty-five. I'm thirty-four."

She already knew that. His information was on the Tate Luxury Home website.

He looked her up and down. "You went to school, and even got a master's, which means you probably didn't leave academia until you were twenty-six. You've already stated that you can't imagine living anywhere else. I know you've been here two years because the museum's website says when you were hired. That makes you twenty-eight."

"You're right."

In the distance, Jilly laughed, an echoing sound soon joined by her father's baritone. Emily spun around and muttered, "You may be right about those two, also."

"They seem to get along, have the same interests," Donovan observed.

"She's nothing like my mother."

"Your mother's the one in the portrait above the entrance to the main dining room. Right?"

"I was four in that portrait, just turned."

"So, that's one of the last family portraits?"

"It was the very last. She died two months later from a very aggressive form of cancer."

"She must really have been something for your father to stay single all these years. It's been twenty-four years."

Emily hadn't really thought about that. There'd

been a time, very brief, when her father had taken Jane's mother out. Patti de la Rosa had been single, with a daughter—who happened to be Eva's best friend. What Emily remembered was Patti stepping in when they needed costumes for school pageants and such. Jacob had a habit of hiring his buddies to work the ranch. Both Cook and Harold Mull, their head wrangler and foreman, were ex-rodeo buddies. Often, the hands they hired were sons of Jacob's friends or troubled youth.

Their dad was even known to hire an ex-con or two. If he knew their history and that a helping hand, a step up, might make a difference.

None of the above knew how to sew an angel dress or make wings. Patti had stepped in. Pretty soon she was an employee.

"Jilly does like horses," Emily murmured to herself.

Donovan nodded.

"Nothing like my mother," Emily repeated, this time trying to convince herself.

"What was your mother like?" Donovan walked over and sat down beside her, this time sitting closer. She could feel his warmth, imagine the way his cheek would feel under her palm.

"My mom was a lot like me—short, slender, brown skinned and strong."

"I could tell that from the portrait."

Emily thought for a moment before allowing, "Maybe. I've always thought I was a mixture."

Growing up, she'd often studied her sisters. It was true, Emily did look the most like Naomi. She'd gotten Naomi's height as well as her coloring and hair. But, where her mother was all angles, compact, what her dad called lithe, Emily was soft. She'd constantly battled the extra fifteen to twenty pounds that wanted to find a home on her not-so-slight frame. Elise was the daughter who'd inherited her mother's athletic ability. She had climbed her first tree at three, had gone on two-hour-long trail rides at four and now could eat a large pizza by herself and not gain so much as an ounce.

There were times that neither Eva nor Emily thought much of the middle child. It was called sibling rivalry.

"I'm a fixer like her dad," Emily said. "And the keeper of tales like my mother."

She had no memories of her mother's voice, scent or even touch.

All she had were the tales, nearly all of them secondhand. Eva had shared a few, what a twelve-year-old girl remembered. Things like going to the state fair and to movies. That was about all Emily really knew. Oh, there were a few vague memories of being at a swimming pool in shallow water and swimming toward a woman who was an arm's length away. She also remembered sitting in the backseat of the car, kicking her feet and singing. Sometimes Emily imagined seeing a dark-haired woman turn and smile, but usually she accepted that that was what she wanted to remember, not an actual event.

"You've seen the brown, orange and beige woven blanket we have on display in the lobby."

"The one in the big glass case?"

"My mother made it. It's the only one she kept. All the others she gave away. Dad said she'd have made one for each of us for our weddings, but one day she had a stomachache, the next day she went to the doctor and the same day she went into the hospital. After that, I remember going into their bedroom, my mom and dad's, and seeing her lying there. All I remember is a white blanket and I could see her nose."

Donovan nodded but didn't say anything.

She stood, wiping the pieces of bark and resin from the back of her jeans. The day was heating up.

"I would have liked to meet your mother," he said.

"She was quite a lady." What Emily didn't add was that her mother—who'd driven her to preschool, stayed late so Emily could swing on the playground and watched *My Pretty Pony* on television every single night—hadn't really returned home from the hospital. No, a healthy, active mom had checked in and a mere shell had checked out.

Emily felt tears in her eyes, but she didn't know who to feel sorry for. Herself, for what

she'd lost, or Donovan, for the family he thought-
lessly neglected.

There was so much about him to like. His semi-
short brown hair with waves. The way his eye-
brows arched over hazel eyes that seemed to see
more than they should. How his nose was a bit
crooked, as if it had been broken. His mouth was
perfect.

And, he had so much to offer: talent, conversation, adventure. He just didn't understand the concept of having a home, establishing roots. He was
like the seeds cast on rocky, shallow soil. They
grew, got scorched and withered.

It was a flaw she neither understood nor forgave.

Chapter Ten

After the trail ride, Emily showered and headed out the door. She'd left Donovan to his own devices. He knew how to unsaddle a horse, how to find his way to breakfast and how to get together with her father for the first baby steps toward building Tinytown. She'd let him distract her *way* too much.

First on her agenda was walking through the museum. She'd not made it there yesterday.

Everything was in its rightful place. She said a silent prayer of thanks.

Heading for the barn, she went for the room where she'd stored the remnants of the Majestic. The sign took up the most space. She'd acquired it for free. If she could get it plugged in, it would sparkle like a disco ball on steroids. The wagon wheels, too, had been a giveaway. They weren't really wagon wheels, so they basically were curved wood that probably wasn't strong enough to support a baby carriage. A Tupperware box held keys with large plastic tags with room numbers stamped large enough so the guest staying two rooms over could see. She also had the key cubbie, as well as three guest registers.

They'd cost money. One had a signature from the guitar player of Elvis's backup band. One of the registers, the oldest, had at least two hundred signatures—all different—from Mr. and Mrs. Smith. No first names.

She also had artwork, much of it by Apache Creek locals no longer living. Most of their families were still around. One sure way to get people to visit a museum was to make it personal.

Heading inside, she paused by a display stating On Loan from the Family of Naomi Humestewa.

It had been a long time since she'd really talked about her mother to anyone. Her dad always got quiet when she brought Naomi up, eventually making some excuse to walk away. Elise remembered some, but she'd always been the sister out and about, doing things, usually alongside their dad. She'd had the least time to share Naomi memories. Eva, though, remembered quite a bit and willingly shared it. She'd inherited their mother's nurturing genes as well as her talent at the loom. All Emily could do was create knots, unintentional ones.

This whole section came from Emily's family. There was pottery, along with altarpieces, ceremonial garb, fetishes, masks and headdresses. They were not trophies, and many of her family members believed they should not be on display. The artifacts didn't belong here. But Emily wanted to use them to teach the museum's visitors the Hopi culture and charm.

Before she had time to do much more than dust, her cell sounded and a breathless Elise said, "I just got a call from Two Mules. One of my kids fell from a horse and broke her collarbone. She's asking for me. It's Bernice Sinquah, and she's scared to death that her parents will tell her she can't compete anymore."

Emily knew Elise's flock of kids, as they came once a week, during the school year, and practiced in Cooper's backyard.

"She's the one with the scholarship and the hovering parents?"

"That's her."

"When will you be back?"

"I don't know. Oh, and FYI, I've scheduled Dad for a meeting with a lawyer this Wednesday. I need you to support me when he protests."

"I'll do my best." Emily thought it would be interesting to see who won the battle of wills when it came to getting Jacob to see the lawyer. "Last I heard, he was trusting the Lord to take care of him. And, if I remember correctly, you're the one who said with no witness, no proof of a crime and no fingerprints on the knife, Dad wasn't a suspect."

"The Lord is taking care of him." Elise sounded somewhat guarded. "But, yesterday at church, Sam was very careful to avoid me."

"Really?" Emily hadn't noticed. Maybe because she'd been looking at the door, hoping Donovan might walk through.

"Last time Sam avoided anyone, according to Eva, it was when he arrested Jesse."

"I think you're overreacting," Emily said.

"I think Johnny Law is keeping certain finds to themselves."

"You don't trust Sam?" Emily queried.

"I don't trust the badge. Last time I spoke with the lawyer, she didn't think she'd be able to meet with Dad until next week. She called about twenty minutes ago to tell me she had a cancellation."

"I guess that's good." Emily would like to think it was God working in their favor.

Elise, ever the worrier, said, "I really think we should be prepared for anything. If I have to, I'll get Eva to help."

Right now, nine months pregnant with Jacob Hubrecht's first grandbaby, Eva pretty much got whatever Eva wanted.

Headed back into her office, she had two things she wanted to do. Check her phone for messages and search the internet for Russell Dairy Farm. She decided her phone would be the quickest.

She was wrong.

The first message was from one of the trustees, Darryl Feeney, who must have called while she was busy. He wanted the museum's June account records. An ex-banker who worried about the museum's finances more than anything else, Feeney often predicted gloom and doom. Emily frowned. June still had a few more days on its calendar. He'd never asked for a report before the end of the month.

The next message was from Donovan. He sounded excited, telling her he'd had an idea about Tinytown and to call him the minute she got back to the ranch.

She pulled the computer keyboard closer and searched for Russell Dairy Farm, but before she had a chance to even look at the first entry, a carful of at least six visitors showed up. She gave a tour. When she finished, her cell phone rang. Eva, sounding out of breath, said, "Dad was at the front desk doing a booking when Sam Miller drove up. He asked Dad to come down to the station. Dad's not arrested. They just want him to come in and answer some questions."

"He's already gone? Why didn't you go with him?"

"I wanted to! Then Jesse offered to go with him, but instead he's driving me to the hospital. My back hurts and it's so bad I can't even sit down. I feel like something's going to break."

"I'll go. Did you call Elise?"

"I just got off the phone with her. She's calling

that lawyer she knows in Phoenix. She tried calling Dad but he's not picking up. She wants you
to tell him to keep quiet and wait for counsel."

"Like Dad will do that."

"I know. Both Harold and Cook offered to go,
but they'd probably wind up arrested for disor-
derly conduct." Eva let out a moan, and in the
background, Emily could hear Jesse saying,
"Come on. Let's get going."

"Donovan drove Dad to the station," Eva finished.

Emily hit the end button and quickly made a
sign that said Be Back Soon before heading out
the door. Her father was bluster and backbone,
which didn't always go over well with the police.
When Sam turned him over to one of the other
officers, her dad could get himself into trouble.

She started the engine and backed out of the
parking lot before she had the driver's side door
all the way closed.

Apache Creek's small police station was in the
center of town. Emily had been in it only once,
back when she was a Girl Scout earning a badge.
She'd refused to go into one of the cells and instead had listened to a cop talking about an arrest.

He'd not known she was listening.

Later, when she shared the story with the other
Girl Scouts, they'd all been enthralled. One phone
call from a parent complaining about too much
detail stopped that story cold.

She parked next to Donovan's truck and hurried out. Pushing open the front doors, she walked into a beige waiting room with ugly green chairs and too many magazines. Who could read when a loved one might be in trouble? Not Donovan, who stood and said, "They took him about five minutes ago. He said he didn't need me."

"Thanks for coming with him. For driving, I mean."

An officer at the front desk, on the phone, held up a finger for her to wait. She wanted to jump over the counter and tell him her dad was more important than any phone call, but she'd been raised better than that. Still, she couldn't sit; she wanted to pace.

Donovan started for her, but she held up her hand. All it would take was a single touch, and she'd start crying.

They were interrogating her dad. Her dad. There were two other people sitting in the waiting room. She didn't want to disturb them, so she looked at the wanted posters on the bulletin board and studied the photographs of officers present and past. Donovan walked with her.

She paused in front of the portrait of an Apache Creek officer who'd died in the line of duty.

"James Shingoitewa," she said. "That's a Hopi name, but I've never heard of him." His face looked somewhat familiar.

"Usually there's a news article, plaque or something." Donovan said.

"Miss?" The officer was off the phone and beckoning.

"I'm Emily Hubrecht. I'm here to be with my father."

"He's with the chief right now. Have a seat, and he'll be out shortly."

Emily had dealt with the police a few times in South Dakota. She knew they always tried to keep a level of control.

"No, I'd like you to tell him I'm here, and see if he'd like me to join him. I'd also like to give him the name of his lawyer. Unless you'd rather deny him the right to confer with legal representation?"

The officer didn't roll his eyes, but Emily could tell he wanted to.

"Impressive," Donovan murmured.

A minute later, she was escorted into a small gray windowless office. A man in a suit stood and held out a hand. "I'm Dan Decker. Captain. We've been asking your father a few questions. So far, he's cooperated."

"Dad," Emily urged. "Elise has a lawyer she wants you to talk to. This can wait. We want to make sure that—"

"It's Billy Wilcox," her dad said.

"What?"

Captain Decker leaned forward. "The skeleton

you helped excavate. Thanks to dental records, we know it's Billy Wilcox, son of your neighbor Karl Wilcox."

Donovan's phone sounded. He grabbed it, feeling somewhat guilty that it rang in a police station, but that was foolish. His whole life he'd never been in one. He was pretty impressed with the way Emily marched in, took the front desk sergeant to task and then was whisked away to rescue her father.

Not that Jacob needed rescuing. The man had nerves of steel. His only comment about being taken in for questioning during the drive over was *Makes life more interesting*.

"Hello," he said as he answered his phone.

The door to the police station opened and Jilly Greenhouse came in. "Where's Jacob?"

Donovan put up a finger. Something about his face must have warned her. He got the idea that Jilly wasn't one who believed in waiting.

"Donovan," came Jesse Campbell's voice, "is Emily with you?"

"I'm in the waiting room, and she's in with whoever's questioning her dad."

"Where's Jacob?" Jilly mouthed.

Jesse muttered, "She must have her cell phone off."

"Why?"

"Because she's not answering!" Jesse's tone clearly conveyed that Donovan's lightbulb was dim.

"I mean," Donovan said, "why do you need her?"

"Eva's in labor."

Donovan almost dropped the phone. "Eva's in labor? You're kidding."

Jilly plopped down next to him. "Give me the phone."

Around the Lost Dutchman Ranch, Jesse wasn't known for his sense of humor. He was a stand-up guy who took care of his own. Donovan had been impressed when he'd heard about Jesse's background. He'd never have guessed the man to be an ex-con.

"Eva wants her dad," Jesse said. "I told her Jacob would be here in forty-five minutes. You'll see to that."

From anyone else, that might have been a question.

"Yes." Donovan handed his phone to Jilly and went to the front desk. "I need to speak with the young lady who went back a few minutes ago."

"Sorry, they can't be interrupted right now." The desk sergeant didn't look up from the report he was reading.

Donovan thought for a moment. He had no clue what copspeak would get him, what he even wanted. Instead, he tried the truth. "I just got a call from Jacob Hubrecht's son-in-law. Jacob's oldest daughter just went in labor with his first grandchild. Let me repeat that in case it's not clear. First. Grandchild. I just promised I'd get him to the hospital."

The cop frowned.

"Babies don't wait," Jilly said, coming to stand beside him.

"Just a minute." The cop disappeared down a hallway. A moment later, a door slammed open. Emily flew down the hall, Jacob a few steps behind her. Captain Decker followed behind them.

"Let me know when you're available to continue this conversation," he called to Jacob's retreating figure.

"Anytime. I've nothing to hide." With that, Jacob followed Jilly out the door. He had his cell phone out and spoke loudly into it. "That's right. Eva's having the baby. What? I'm glad you're there. Here's what I want you to do. Make a sign. Say that the owner's first grandchild is about to be born. The restaurant is closed for the night. Call the minister. His wife said she'd help out if we needed her. Wait for her to get there, tell her who's checking in, and then you and Cook get over here."

"Dad's talking to Harold," Emily supplied. "Everyone will want to be at the hospital."

Jacob was still talking away as he got into

Jilly's car. Something about watching a tall cowboy fold his body into a Fiat 500 made Donovan smile.

Looking over, Donovan saw that Emily was already halfway into her truck. He'd either be following, riding along or heading back to the ranch to his empty room. He'd always done well on multiple-choice questions.

"Wait."

He climbed into the passenger side, put on his seat belt and then watched as Apache Creek's Main Street sailed by. "Good thing all the cops are back at the station wondering if they did the right thing by letting your dad go."

She shot him a dirty look. "They were just questioning him. They couldn't keep my dad. He didn't do anything."

"Why did they bring him in today? What changed?"

She hesitated, just a moment, and said, "The remains have been identified as Billy Wilcox."

"The bedroom with the posters on the wall. Karl's boy." Donovan whistled. "Finally home."

"What's curious," Emily continued, "is that the medical examiner agreed with my assessment that we had a male between the ages of twenty-five and forty."

"And Billy…?"

"Disappeared when he was seventeen."

"Wow," Donovan said. "So, it means either he

lived out in the middle of nowhere, because unless I'm wrong, that's what Ancient Trails was back then. Or he came back."

Emily tightened her grip on the steering wheel. "I don't know what the area looked like thirty years ago. Maybe my dad would know."

"There was nothing there before we started building. It was hard, packed soil. I found no evidence of a structure. No rusted nails, slate, spent coal. If he'd built some kind of—"

"He didn't. When he disappeared, the search parties spent days canvassing the area. They'd have searched there. Plus, if my dad's correct, Karl actively searched up until ten or fifteen years ago, when it was just too hard for him to continue. And, where you're building has always been a popular place for horseback riders."

"When Billy disappeared," Donovan mused, "did a horse go missing?"

"What? I don't know. That's a good question. If he had a horse, he could have gone deeper into the wilderness, survived off the land. It's been done before, and the Superstition Mountains have caves and year-round vegetation."

Donovan shook his head. "It's easy to sit here and suppose, but what kid wants to be so totally alone, especially so close to home and comforts?"

"We've always had tourists complaining about their stuff going missing. Food, clothes, books."

Donovan shook his head. "I know I brought

it up, but now that I really think about it, not a chance."

"There are many kinds of hermits," she pointed out.

"And this one died with a knife next to his body." Donovan was smart enough not to mention the initials.

"Okay," she said after a moment. "Then, let's assume he came back. How did he wind up there? Was he walking, heading for Karl's place, or did he call someone and Ancient Trails is where they met?"

"The body's been there a bit longer than thirty years. If Billy was alive today he'd be fifty-five. So, let's assume he was twenty-four."

"A year younger than the supposed twenty-five to forty," Emily agreed. Then, she hit her hand on the steering wheel. "I cannot believe I'm having this gruesome talk while driving to the hospital to welcome a niece or nephew."

Donovan thought about it for a moment. "It probably has to do with where you were and what you were talking about before Jesse called me."

"I'm going to be an aunt," Emily said, awe in her voice.

They'd long left the confines of Apache Creek. For a few miles, there was nothing. Now they were in the big city of Phoenix, spread out, and Donovan noted that they'd passed a street called Mc-

Dowell at least four times. "Do you know where you're going?"

"Nearest hospital is here in Phoenix. We've a clinic in Apache Creek. Plans are in the works to build a hospital."

"Want me to drive?"

She looked at him and then back at the road. "No. I know where the hospital is. We'll be there in five minutes."

"I wasn't worried."

Her driving was the least of his worries. What he needed to worry about was the fact that he willingly jumped into her truck to head to the hospital to celebrate the birth of a baby whose mother he'd known for only a little more a month and a half.

He was getting entirely too involved in a family that wasn't his.

"There's a parking place."

Before he could offer an opinion about whether the spot was too narrow, which it was, she'd parked the truck. He edged open the door and squeezed out. Not being a fool, he didn't comment.

She headed for the entrance in a half jog, half hop movement. Halfway to the door, she whipped out her phone and punched in a text, waited a moment and then said, "Jesse says to come up to the fourth-floor waiting room."

"I guess that means the baby's not born."

Her phone pinged, and she paused to read the next message.

"Maybe we could stop by the second floor first."

"Why?"

"Karl's here, too. Seems the news about his son was too much for him."

Chapter Eleven

Emily sat in the chair closest to Karl and took out her cell phone. Quickly she texted Jesse: What's happening? Having baby yet?

Not yet was his quick response.

Donovan pulled a chair over next to her. Feeling relieved, she took his strong fingers in hers, feeling their warmth, and tightened her grip before saying a prayer. She prayed for Karl, for Eva and ended with Billy.

Donovan whispered an "Amen" but didn't add anything. After a few moments, Emily said, "Elise needs to be here. She and Cooper's family, especially Garrett. They've pretty much adopted Karl as their own."

"I got that impression."

Emily quickly sent a text to Cooper, updating him on Karl's status. To Donovan, she said, "Up until Cooper's little brother started working with Karl, not just his place but Karl, himself, was run-down."

"I like his ranch. It reminds me of the past. I don't think we want to lose all the places that remind us progress was created on the back of hard work and dreams."

He surprised her. It might have been the most poetic thing he'd said. And, coming from the man who'd designed and built the Baer home, it was contradictory.

Confusing.

Who was the real Donovan Russell?

Karl moaned a little, turning restlessly and then settling in the exact same position he'd started at.

"Karl's doing pretty well, considering he's in his eighties. Last time he was here, the doctor said he had a strong heart, good lungs and all that. Back then, his biggest enemy was the will to live. He doesn't have that problem anymore."

"How do you know?"

"Because not a day goes by when he doesn't get a visit from either one of the girls, Cooper's family or Jilly Greenhouse. Then, too, at least four or five times a week he comes to the ranch to eat."

Her phone pinged the arrival of a text from Cooper: On our way.

"That's nice," Donovan argued, "but—"

"But, most important, he came back to church. Doesn't miss a service. I've never seen him happier."

"And you think church is the number one reason for that change, not the people giving him their time?"

"Absolutely."

Donovan started to say something, obviously thought better of it and said, "He looks good for being in his eighties."

"He still works the land. Mostly telling or showing Garrett what to do."

Karl moaned again.

"I'm here, Karl. Do you need the nurse? Just squeeze my fingers. I'll call someone."

Karl didn't squeeze, but his fingers felt cold and so terribly thin. She knew he was eating. Oh, never a whole hamburger, but he'd put away half. Her dad said not to worry. That it didn't take as much coal to move a train that didn't go far.

Whatever that meant.

Donovan stretched his legs out, clearly uncomfortable, and looked around the sterile room. Emily made a mental note to call the church secretary. In two days' time, Karl would have enough cards to fill all the shelf space.

"It has to be hard," Donovan said, interrupting her musing, "having just one child, and that child disappointing you."

"Or maybe," Emily said, "knowing that you disappointed your child."

"What makes you think that?"

"Something Elise told me. She said Karl always blamed himself for Billy running away, something about Billy being bullied and Karl telling him to man up."

"That's what my dad would have told me."

"I think the type of bullying going on has changed in the last decade or two. I'm not sure what Billy would have dealt with in the seventies, but I know the bullying I witnessed the past ten years. It needs to be stopped. No tolerance."

"You weren't bullied, were you?"

Emily was a bit impressed. Donovan brought his legs in and almost stood. He looked ready to take on the world on her behalf, or at least the bullies of the world.

"No, I was left alone, but I had Elise as a big sister, and my dad was at the school a lot."

She saw him mentally doing the math. "Elise was in school when you were?"

"I was a freshman when she was a senior. But, really, my dad ran the after-school rodeo club. There wasn't a detail of my life he didn't know. If someone bullied me, one of the kids in the club would have told him. That's a great way to deter bullies."

Donovan grinned. "I can just see your dad marching into a classroom, picking a student up by his shirtfront and shaking him."

"No, if it were serious, my dad would have requested the bully either be expelled or, more likely, he'd have made it mandatory that the bully be forced to join the rodeo club. Most bullies aren't into team sports that don't involve knocking people down. I was left alone, but I witnessed plenty."

A nurse breezed in, picked up the chart at the end of Karl's bed, made a notation and then hustled over to adjust a knob on the wall by Karl's pillow.

When the nurse finished, she said, "Are you Karl's family?"

"Close enough," Emily said. "I'm Emily Hubrecht. My dad is Jacob Hubrecht. He's listed as the emergency contact. How's Karl doing?"

"We're keeping him comfortable." The nurse patted Karl's shoulder gently and smiled. "The doctor should be around later this afternoon. He can tell you more. Will your father be available?"

"Yes, let me give you my cell phone number. My dad's on the fourth floor. My oldest sister is having a baby."

"Right now?"

"She's in labor."

The nurse walked to a dry-erase board and wrote down the number Emily shared. Then, she said, "Mr. Wilcox will probably be out for another two hours, if that helps any. I'll leave the doctor a note."

Standing, Emily said, "If Karl needs anything, let me know."

"I'll call you if he so much as burps," the nurse promised.

Free, Emily flew from the room with Donovan at her heels. At first, she turned the wrong way, but Donovan gently guided her back to the elevator and pushed the up button, giving her a look that told her he didn't trust her to go the right direction. When the door opened to a corridor of color, with painted balloons on the walls and stuffed animals displayed under glass, Emily felt her knees start to buckle.

"I'm going to be an aunt," she whispered.

In the distance, a baby cried. The scent of talcum powder and something else, maybe vanilla or coconut, lingered in the air. Laughter echoed down the hall. Emily followed it until she came to a waiting room so filled with people that she had no place to sit.

"Emily!" Timmy hurried toward her, crawling over Cook's feet and practicing falling. "I held Eva's hand in the car and told her to squeeze whenever she got a pain."

"I hope she didn't squeeze too hard."

"She did," Timmy shared, "but I didn't complain."

"That's what family is for," Emily told him.

Timmy stayed by her side, which didn't surprise Emily. In the family, she was the closest one not only to his age, but to his size. He might be feeling a bit overwhelmed.

While Donovan knelt next to Harold Mull, the ranch's foreman, Emily hurried over to her father and asked, "You heard anything?"

"Jesse texts every few minutes but only says that she's in labor. I don't know if the contractions are getting closer together or what."

"When he stops texting," Jilly said, "you'll know it's close to time. He'll be too busy becoming a daddy to care about us out here."

Emily felt tears form. She'd hoped that Eva would ask her to go into the delivery room with her, but she opted for only Jesse. She'd taken a children's book, one Emily recommended, called *Love You Forever.* Jesse had orders to read it should the pain get too bad.

Emily's cell sounded. She looked at the number and held up a finger to her dad. "Hello."

"It's Cooper. Garrett, Mom and I are down in Karl's room. Anything happening up there?"

"No, is Karl still asleep?"

"Yup."

"The nurse wrote my number on the dry-erase board," Emily said. "She said she'd call if anything happened."

"I'll add my number and come up. Is Elise back yet?"

"No, I'm not even sure what time she left Two Mules."

"She left when she found out your dad was being questioned by the police."

"Then she should be here by now." Emily felt the tug of worry. The drive between Two Mules and the next small town was isolated and downtrodden. If she'd broken down, it would take hours, but she'd have called."

"She not answering her phone?" Emily asked.

"What's going on?" Jacob asked, picking up on Emily's concern.

"Cooper wants to know where Elise is."

Jacob took the phone from Emily. "Elise texted me that she wound up donating blood for her student. They wouldn't let her drive right after. She should be on her way now."

Emily couldn't hear what Cooper said, but Jacob responded with, "She didn't want to worry you while you were helping Garrett at ASU."

"She could have called me instead of making me worry," Emily grumbled.

"Worry doesn't add a single day to your life," Jacob said, handing the phone to Emily.

After she ended the call, Jacob said, "I forgot to ask him how Karl's doing."

"You can ask me. Donovan and I were just down there. He's sleeping. I gave the nurse my number. If something comes up, she'll call."

"I told the captain he was ten times a fool for letting a stranger break the news to Karl. When it comes to Billy, Karl never stopped believing. Finding out the boy was so close yet…"

Jilly leaned forward. "Shhh, not everyone knows yet, and this probably isn't the time or the place.

As if to prove her point, two more people pushed into the waiting room.

"Did we miss anything?" Eva's best friend, Jane de la Rosa, hurried over to Emily. She held a basketful of blankets and sleepers.

"No, she's still in labor," Jacob said.

Jane's mother joined them, making sure to stand next to Jacob before saying, "Exciting day?" The words were upbeat, but Emily didn't miss the look Patti de la Rosa gave Jilly. It had been years since her father and Patti looked more than twice at each other, but Jane always claimed that her mother still wished things had worked out.

"One of the best," Jacob agreed.

Looking around the waiting room, Emily had to agree. Harold and Donovan were laughing about something. Cook was looking through the basket Jane had brought in. Already, Cooper, Garrett and their mother were crowding through the door.

Emily wasn't sure if Cooper and Garrett knew that the body had been identified as Billy Wilcox. She doubted it.

Emily wasn't even sure if Elise knew.

Patti stood on one side of Jacob, Jilly on the other. Emily had to admire Jilly. She didn't look as if she cared a whit what Patti was doing.

Patti, on the other hand, seemed a little frantic in her actions, her voice a little too loud. "You've never said whether Eva's having a boy or a girl."

The room did quiet. After all, it was the question of the moment. No matter how many times she'd been questioned, Eva hadn't shared whether she was having a boy or girl. Jesse had been no help when he'd been asked. He'd just shrugged and said if his wife wanted the family to know, she'd do the telling.

"I'm not sure," Jacob admitted.

"I'm sure you'd like a boy," Patti observed. "You've only had girls. You'd enjoy a grandson."

Jacob looked a bit surprised. "What do you mean, I've only had girls? I've got one of the best grandsons in the world. Timmy can outride most teenagers and he's only been on a horse for the last three years. He's one of the best dinner companions I've got. And you should see him create a Lego world. He's all the boy I need. Should Eva have a boy, both Timmy and I will help take care of him."

Across the room, Timmy looked up. He seemed to grow in that moment, mature. Emily, already feeling sentimental because of Eva, couldn't swallow.

In truth, she couldn't remember ever being more proud of her father.

It occurred to her that everyone she loved most was at the hospital. Except for Elise.

Her eyes sought out and found Donovan.

He wasn't smiling.

When the clock signaled eight, most everyone headed downstairs to eat. Jacob ate with one hand holding his fork and the other holding his cell phone. With Emily settled next to him, Donovan tried to figure out just exactly how he'd gotten involved in all the family dynamics.

He felt at home with the entire extended family.

He sure hadn't felt that way when he was with Olivia and her friends and family. He'd always escaped at the earliest possible moment. Tonight, he didn't even mind eating cafeteria food while discussion swirled around him.

"I think if it's a boy, he should be named Harold," Harold said. The man personified a cowboy in a Jack Palance sort of way. His hair was dirty blond, thick and shaggy. His face was permanently tanned, lined and partly obscured by a shaggy mustache.

Donovan immediately pictured a tiny baby in a cowboy hat with a red kerchief around his neck.

"Really?" Jacob said. "You think that Harold is a better name than Jacob?"

"Not enough Harolds in the world."

"There are three Jacobs in my class," Timmy announced. "One goes by Jake."

"Jacob could be the middle name," Patti suggested. "Then, Eva and Jesse could name him whatever they want."

"Eva could name him David after me," Cook offered.

"I didn't know David was your first name," Timmy burst out.

"It's true," Jacob said. "No one knows your name is David."

"I do now," Patti laughed.

"We're not even sure it's a boy," Jacob said.

"It's a boy," Harold said.

"I'm named after Mom," Jane said.

When everyone looked at Patti, she nodded. "My first name is Jane. I've always gone by Patricia because my mom was Jane. It got too confusing. That's another reason why I think Jacob should be a middle name. You guys have way too many *J* names. Jacob, Jesse, Jilly—"

"Jane," Jane put in.

Conversation continued with the naming game changing from half-serious to not a chance. About the time that Timmy suggested Eva should name the baby Luke Skywalker, Donovan nudged Emily. "You need to eat. Elise will be here any minute."

Her plate was full. She was as bad as her father, constantly looking at her cell.

"Oh, I didn't tell you. She's texted a moment ago. She's up in Karl's room."

"Does she know?" Donovan asked.

"Know what?" Harold asked, reminding Donovan that families were a lot like small towns. If you wanted to keep a secret, you didn't share it unless you were two states away.

A look passed between Emily and Jacob. As

if sensing the seriousness, everyone at the table leaned forward.

"I wasn't told to keep this to myself, and seeing how Karl collapsed—"

"The two are connected?" Patti guessed.

Jane and Cook both gasped. Harold looked thoughtful, but Patti leaned forward, figuring it out before Jacob could respond. "The skeleton was Billy Wilcox," Patti gasped.

Jacob nodded. "His dental records prove it. The only thing we can't figure is how or why. He was seventeen when he ran away. Both DNA and dental records prove it's Billy."

"How did he die?" Harold asked.

"I'm not sure they know yet."

"It wasn't a blow to the head," Emily said.

Almost immediately, Donovan could tell, she wanted her words back. Looking around the table at each and every person, he watched the levels of comprehension.

"So, they think he was murdered?" Patti asked.

"They're not sure."

"Then why did they take you in for questioning again today?" Harold said indignantly.

"You went in for questioning again today?" Patti echoed.

"They're still playing around with the knife and my initials."

"Probably a dozen knives with those initials," Cook said.

"And if you lose yours," Jacob joked, "you'll never get it back because no one knows who D.C. is."

That got a few chuckles. Emily leaned back, looking relieved, and Donovan put a hand on her knee. She didn't move it, just glanced at him, something akin to fear in her eyes.

"It will be all right," he mouthed.

"There's not one thing to connect you to Billy Wilcox," Cook declared.

Donovan didn't miss the look shared by both Harold and Patti. Neither did anyone else, apparently.

"What?" Cook asked.

"It's nonsense," Jacob said.

"It is," Patti agreed, "but nonsense has gotten more than one man in trouble."

Jilly said softly, "What is it, Jacob?" Donovan hadn't noticed until that moment that she had her hand on his shoulder.

"Oh, it's nothing. I told the cops. When Naomi was in high school, she dated Billy a bit. First time I met her was at the rodeo. She was a bit of a thing, only sixteen. If you'd have told me I'd be marrying her, I'd have fallen off my horse."

"So Billy didn't like you?" Jilly queried.

"I don't think he even knew me!" Jacob protested.

"She stopped dating him because she liked you?" Emily asked.

Never again would Donovan complain about small towns being boring.

"If she did, I wasn't aware of it. Yes, I knew that I'd sat with a pretty girl at the cowboy supper. Yes, I knew she'd looked at me adoringly—"

Patti snorted.

Jacob gave her a dirty look. "—at the carnival after we rode the Ferris wheel. But honestly, I was a twenty-three-year-old buck, and the sixteen-year-old girl was wet behind the ears."

"Was Billy at the rodeo?" Cook asked.

"Not that I know of. Patti, do you know?"

"Probably. The rodeo was something we all went to. Most of us competed. I won the barrel racing event." She gleefully added, "I won all three runs. I always said it was because Naomi was distracted. Thanks, Jacob."

"Wish I could remember."

"You were busy with other things. Billy wasn't a competitor, though. He'd go to watch."

She smiled and suddenly Donovan saw where Jane got her beauty. Clearly, the memories were good.

"Billy looked like a cowboy, walked like a cowboy and all that," Patti remembered, "but he'd fall off the horse even if the beast was standing still."

"Not much fun," Emily said.

Jacob nodded.

"That was the rodeo," Patti went on, "where

a stray firework shot into the crowd and set Gramma Hamm's purse on fire."

"Mike Hamm's great-grandmother," Jacob supplied.

"And my gramma," Patti said. "I've been a de la Rosa so long that people tend to forget that once upon a time I was Hamm. Oh, but Gramma was mad. You'd thought she had a million dollars in that purse. She spent the next two years complaining that her new driver's license made her look older."

"She made our wedding cake," Jacob added to the story.

In a way, Donovan figured, listening to these two—with both Cook and Harold adding bits along the way about other rodeos and people—was like the town of Apache Creek spreading its arms and surrounding him.

Before, he always shrugged off any attempt someone made at grounding him. He didn't feel that way now.

"That was the best rodeo ever," Patti ended her story.

"I enjoyed it, too. Strange thing is," he added, "that's the rodeo where I won the knife, and they carved my initials in the handle."

Chapter Twelve

It was after nine when everyone returned to the maternity floor's waiting room. Another smaller family was in the corner. The vivid blue sky had turned dark, and the ward had a silence that spelled the end of the shift for nurses, mommies and babies.

The only noise on the floor came from the waiting room.

Emily settled into a corner chair and responded no baby yet to five texts in a row, while Timmy whined about being bored across the room, kicking his feet against the bottom of his chair. The other family looked his way. They didn't seem too excited about the noise. Emily wanted to remind them that in ten years whatever little bundle they welcomed tonight would be a lot like Timmy.

"All right if I turn the television on?" Cook asked. "I want to watch the news."

No one said yes.

In ten minutes' time, Jane and Patti took off. Emily promised to text them the minute she heard anything. Even as they sailed through the door, Patti was looking back at Jilly as if wondering why the other woman seemed inclined to stay.

Or maybe not wondering but clearly seeing— like Emily was.

Cook and Harold headed back to the ranch, taking Timmy with them. He wanted to stay, but the confines of a single room had started wearing on his ten-year-old energy level. Cook had the same exact antsy expression. Emily knew that the two would engage in a Nerf battle when they got home.

Jacob wasn't willing to leave. He'd parked himself in a chair and was reading the newspaper with Jilly looking over his shoulder, commenting on the presidential hopefuls and state of Arizona's education system.

Donovan sat next to Emily, texting on his phone while his feet stuck out in the aisle again. He'd already had to move them twice so people could pass by.

"I think I'm going to regret not knowing Great-Gramma Hamm," Donovan said.

"She died before I was born, too. By the way, you were so right about my dad and Jilly. I can't believe I missed it."

"It's pretty easy to figure out that Patti's at-tracted to your dad, too."

"That's not hard to notice. It's part of the reason why she no longer works at the Lost Dutchman. She made a few decisions while working the front desk without consulting Dad. Decisions that only family should have made. Sure surprised us, though, when he let her go. I think we were all expecting him to marry her."

"It would never work." Donovan shook his head.

"Why? How do you know?"

"She's high maintenance."

"And Jilly's not?" Emily said it a little louder than she'd meant to, earning a frown from her father and Jilly mouthing, "I'm not high maintenance."

"Jilly's a different kind of high maintenance. She can take care of herself. Jane's mom would rather someone take care of her."

Elise entered the room then, carrying a plate, and sat across from Emily but didn't start eating.

"Karl's awake. Cooper and Garrett are talking to him. He's crying. I've never seen anything like it. I thought I could stomach anything, but I had to get out of there. You should see Cooper and Garret. They're practically in bed with him, holding him. I think of how Dad might feel if one of us disappeared."

"I don't even want to imagine," Emily responded.

Elise, a social worker for Apache Creek's high

school, always tried to look at life from every angle. "Billy ran away. He made a choice."

Quickly Emily shared everything that was said at the dinner table, especially what Patti de la Rosa had shared.

"Being uncoordinated on a horse is no reason to run away. Family stays together through thick and thin. Running away only makes things worse."

"Patti said something about Billy having a crush on our mom."

Elise looked surprised. "That's a twist."

"When we get home, I want to go through some of the photos. Patti made me think about Mom and the rodeo. Apparently, the rodeo where Mom and Dad met is the one where Dad got the knife."

"Stupid knife."

Silently, Emily agreed. "Still, Dad has his knife. And I'm glad they identified the body. I still can't believe it's Billy Wilcox."

"The doctor came in a little while ago. He said Karl has an anxiety disorder that affects his heart."

"Last time Karl was in the hospital was when Garrett went missing," Emily told Donovan, quickly sharing the story.

"And now today," Elise ended.

"He'll be all right?" Donovan asked.

"Yes. The doctor said Karl might be discharged tomorrow or the day after." Elise put down her untouched plate and went over to sit by her dad. Emily caught the words *stay with us for a while* and *see that Billy has a proper burial.*

Eva was the nurturer. Elise knew how to take care of the important details. Emily felt lost for just a moment and then decided that she knew what to do. She'd long ago started the book about her mother. It had segued into much more, containing the history of the Salado as well as the town of Apache Creek. Billy belonged there, too. She'd see that a whole chapter went to him. She just knew if she looked she could find a picture of both her mother and Billy at a rodeo.

Elise came back and joined them, picking up her cold plate of food and diving in.

Leaning forward, Elise whispered to Emily, "You think eventually, Timmy and the new baby will call Jilly Grandmother?"

"Never."

Donovan agreed. "She's more a Granny Jilly type."

A nurse came to the door but called a name that had the other family jumping up and following her. Elise finished her meal and pulled out her phone. "I'm going to check on Karl and call Bernice's parents to see how she's doing."

"Bernice?" Donovan queried.

"She's the girl who was thrown from her horse earlier today. That's why Elise was in Two Mules. She's in the hospital, too, over in Globe."

Looking over at her dad, Emily noted Jilly's head leaning against his shoulder; Jilly was fast asleep.

"You don't have to stay," Emily told Donovan. "I can give you the keys to my truck. Elise or Jilly will take me home."

"I've been here this long."

Elise chose that moment to return and looked at the two of them as if realizing something. Emily gave the briefest shake of her head. No way did she want Elise playing matchmaker.

"Soooo," Elise said. "Donovan, you're going to be working on Tinytown. How long will that take? And, what's after that?"

"Hard to answer," Donovan admitted. "The contract I've signed with your father gives me the freedom to work on Tinytown between jobs. Right now, I've a good six weeks before my California building begins."

Emily already knew this, but her heart still missed a beat at the words.

Donovan wasn't a permanent kind of guy.

"However, Tate Luxury Homes could send me to help with an existing job site. Or…" He paused.

"Not a chance you'll finish the Baer house?" Elise asked.

It was a question Emily should have posed but didn't. She didn't want to know the answer. If he said yes, she'd struggle with her feelings.

She liked him.

If he said no, she knew that he was temporary in the truest form.

"Baer might have changed his mind now that the remains have been identified and the mystery will die down. But, he's more than spooked about the levels of radon the inspector reported."

"Why didn't you test for radon earlier?" Emily asked. When Donovan first announced why the Baer construction had ceased, she'd researched the radioactive gas, worried that it could harm what she considered a Salado site.

"We did, but apparently the levels increased as building progressed. Baer wanted a basement. He wanted a well dug. Then when the county started putting in pipes, well, we were tampering with the underground. Radon levels spiked as a result."

"And radon is that dangerous?" Elise asked. Emily decided she was too disgruntled to contribute.

She'd been against him building there from day one. He should have listened.

"I've submitted a few drawings for him to consider. Just adding swamp coolers will help if he'd use them. Plus, I'm bringing in a team to assure there are no cracks in the foundation. Based on what Baer has spent, adding a heat recovery ventilator makes sense. If he allows all this, I'll finish the job and his home will be as safe as any other."

"So there's a chance you'll finish?"

Donovan looked at Emily. She saw regret and

maybe some compassion in his eyes. "There's a chance."

"Hmmph."

"My sister," Elise said, "is stubborn."

"Only when it counts," Emily said, sticking up for herself.

"Which is all the time," Elise countered.

Emily's stomach hurt. Maybe it was the events of the day: her dad taken in for questioning, Eva's baby coming, the body being identified, Karl collapsing.

Donovan by her side almost the whole time, which felt so impossibly right.

"I'm looking for Jacob Hubrecht."

Everyone stopped talking and stood, watching the nurse who'd just entered the room.

"I'm Jacob."

"Follow me," said the nurse. "Your daughter wants you."

"How about me?" Emily said. "I'm her sister."

Elise nodded.

But Jacob and the nurse were already out of the room.

"I'm texting Jesse," Elise said.

Emily checked her phone. Who'd said that when Jesse stopped texting, it might mean he was too busy becoming a dad? It had been a while.

Elise started pacing.

Emily collapsed in the chair and looked at the

ceiling. Today might possibly be the longest day of her life. And the one with the most highs and lows!

"The nurse was smiling," Donovan noted.

"How could you tell? She came, she went, no time for questions."

Emily's phone pinged. Come down the hall. Turn left. She turned to share the news, but everyone was gathered around her except Elise, who was already through the waiting room door.

How four adults managed a quiet half jog through the hallway, Emily didn't know. The jog, however, ended at a large window. The same nurse who'd fetched Jacob entered the room. Coming to the window, she held up a dark-haired—all that hair!—sleeping baby.

Even Donovan, Emily noticed, had his nose pressed against the window.

"Beautiful," Jilly breathed.

Then the nurse laid the baby in a bed, and Emily read the name card at the foot.

Naomi Campbell.

Apparently the only one worried about working the next day was Cooper, Elise's fiancé.

Donovan found himself hugging Emily goodbye—feeling very much like he belonged with her—and following Cooper and his younger brother, Garrett, to their car.

Both were amazed that the skeletal remains were Billy Wilcox.

"Mom took it pretty hard," Garrett shared once they were on their way home.

"You told her?" Cooper said.

"She asked why Mr. Hubrecht was taken in for questioning," Garrett defended himself.

The time spent with Emily at the police station seemed like another day, long ago.

After a few minutes, Garrett said, "I wonder if Karl is willing to sell now that he knows for sure Billy won't be coming home."

The thought had crossed Donovan's mind, too.

"No, he won't sell," Cooper said.

"I think he will." Garrett leaned forward. "That place is too much for him, and he needs to be where people can take care of him."

Cooper didn't hesitate to reassure him. "He's doing all right on his own for now."

"But I need to be there helping him. Maybe I—"

"You're going to be in college for the next four years. You'll have to help out summers and holidays. That's growing season anyway."

"No, it's not," Garrett muttered.

Donovan agreed. In Nebraska, summer was growing season. In Arizona, summer was shrivel-up-and-die-from-the-heat season.

"Main crop is cotton. You'll be picking in August."

"I'll never be able to afford a place like Karl's.

I've no savings and when I graduate, I'll be even more in debt. Maybe I shouldn't go—"

Donovan didn't want to tell Garrett how right he was about the cost of a spread like this. No doubt the visit from Randall Tucker was making the boy think and think hard. Smart kid.

"Stop," Cooper said. "We've been over this. College is a necessity, not a choice."

Donovan's parents had been amazed at his desire to go to college. Both had only gone to high school. Both believed that taking over the dairy farm was job security.

"He's right," Donovan spoke up. "College is your number one priority. I had to fight to get into a college, pay my own way and I've never regretted it. A place like this needs someone with good business sense."

Garrett didn't seem willing to discuss the matter any further.

"I went to college on a rodeo scholarship," Cooper shared.

"With Elise."

There seemed to be a bit of hesitation before Cooper answered, "No."

"When did you and Elise meet? You're from here, right?"

"Elise and I were high school sweethearts. It just took us a while to get it right."

Donovan knew that Elise left home at eighteen and hadn't returned until last summer. So far, no one had shared why. In reality, he'd not been curious until now.

Staring out the window, Donovan almost laughed. They were getting closer to Apache Creek. And he knew it not because of the signs on the freeway but because of the landmarks. A giant parking area was to his right—in three or four months it would be home to a flock of snowbirds. To his left was the empty shell used for the Renaissance fair.

Apache Creek was still a small town but thanks to people like Nolan Tate, Randall Tucker and Donovan Russell, it wouldn't be for long.

No wonder locals like Emily and Garrett felt threatened.

Cooper turned onto the freeway and drove through town. Only the convenience store was open. Its parking lot was empty, and a clerk leaned on the counter watching television.

Three buildings down, Cooper pulled into the police station's parking lot and let Donovan out.

"You know," Cooper said, when Donovan started to close the door, "it's not hard to see that you like Emily and she likes you. You need to know, though, if you hurt her in any way, you won't just have her dad to contend with, you'll have me."

"And me," Garrett said from the backseat.

"I don't intend to hurt anyone," Donovan responded.

"You hurt Emily the first day you arrived,

building that big old house out on Ancient Trails Road," Garrett reminded him.

Donovan finished closing the door. Bad enough that others were giving voice to the attraction he was feeling toward Emily, but to be threatened by a high school senior!

Donovan's third night in the cabin was really a morning. It was after midnight when he finally kicked off his shoes and crawled into bed.

Then, he couldn't sleep.

His mind skimmed over the day's events. He'd been dragged along with the Hubrecht family as they oohed and aahed at Naomi, then he'd gone to Eva's room—even though visiting hours were long over. He'd never seen such happiness, not all at once, not so contagious.

Emily positively glowed.

And Donovan had been noticed noticing.

He wondered if Jacob realized what was happening.

Donovan figured that Jacob had enough on his mind. To keep it that way, Donovan didn't dare go back to the hospital. He needed to keep his distance, finish the Tinytown project. Do his job.

He'd start late afternoon tomorrow, since he'd already volunteered to help around the Lost Dutchman while Jacob did Grandpa duties, even taking over a trail ride in the morning. Yes, he'd hobbled around a bit, sore because it had been a while since he'd ridden. Good thing so much had happened yesterday that no one had time to tease him.

If they'd noticed.

When sleep finally came, it offered dreams he didn't want to have, promises he couldn't afford to make.

His alarm rang just before five. He rolled out of bed, dressed, brushed his teeth and hurried—albeit in a still-sore half hobble—to the barn where Harold Mull already had a few horses saddled.

"You've got four riders this morning. One is a family of three. The father rode as a child. Neither the mother or son have ever been on the back of a horse. Pay attention to them. The other is an adult male, average rider. If you think you need help, let me know. I'll call the vet and tell him to come a different day."

Harold probably thought the only reason he wasn't in charge of the ride had to do with a pending visit from the vet. Not so. Jacob shared that while Harold was the best horseman in the state, his people skills were a bit lacking. Meaning he could take a trail ride out, not speak a word except for *don't let the horse lead you* and return to the stables. Most of the Lost Dutchman guests wanted a bit more communication.

Thanks to Emily's storytelling, Donovan could share the area's history and no one would guess he'd only been around a few months.

On the Lost Dutchman, Harold was probably the person Donovan knew least. He seldom sat at a table in the restaurant and shared conversation. He ate and left, preferring to be with the horses. What Donovan did know was that man had rodeoed with Jacob, so they were about the same age. Donovan guessed, just by Harold's appearance, that Harold was older.

Before yesterday's ride, it had been almost twenty years since Donovan worked with a horse. Still, when the guests showed up, almost on time, it felt natural. The ride went without a hitch and, an hour and a half later, Donovan was back at the barn helping Harold loosen cinches and cooling down the horses.

Donovan would never get used to the Arizona heat. It stuck like glue, making him feel as though he was in an oven. Worse, even on a ridiculously early morning ride, the horse underneath him had been a heating coil.

"You go on up to the main house," Harold said. "I'll take care of the grooming."

Donovan figured he could eat three breakfasts. The water and granola bars he'd passed out to the four riders hadn't been filling. They all had grabbed breakfast beforehand, as the brochure suggested. Smart people.

Jacob wasn't around.

"Already at the hospital," Elise supplied without prompting as Donovan headed for the breakfast bar.

"And Emily?"

"She went to work early. Said something about leaving things undone yesterday."

Very few people were in the restaurant. Donovan filled his plate and sat at a table against the back wall. Never had he eaten alone at the Lost Dutchman. From the first day, he'd been surrounded by people who welcomed him. Even back when he was going full steam on the Baer house. Only Emily had raised her pretty little nose in the air and chosen a different table. Unless she was serving him. Then, she didn't say any more than necessary—how hard that must have been for her—and refilled his tea without a smile.

Elise brought over a full saltshaker.

"You're pretty empty this morning," Donovan observed.

"Probably the note posted last night encouraged people to hold off until Eva comes home. When she does, our business will triple. Everyone will want to see the baby, and no one will want to wait until Sunday."

Donovan couldn't even imagine the mind-set that would have a man like Jacob close down his operation because of something so simple, so mundane, as a birth.

He didn't think his dad would have.

Of course, watching the Hubrecht family last night, they didn't view it as mundane.

And in Donovan's dad's defense, he'd see nursing a sick cow to health while his grandson was being born as making sure there'd always be food on the table and a roof over the child's head.

All Donovan's life, he'd wanted to escape a way of life that was so restricting.

What was it he'd heard last night in the waiting room? *Running away only makes things worse.* The context had been Billy Wilcox. It was one piece of a conversation. That Elise said it, and not Emily, didn't lessen the impact.

Was that what he'd done all those years ago? Run away?

He'd thought of it as striking out on an adventure, taking charge of his own life.

For the first time in a long time, Donovan thought about his broken engagement. Had he run away from that, too?

No. The fact that he worked for her father, repaying his debt, swayed in Donovan's favor.

Why was he wrestling with this now? Maybe because he kept comparing the two: Olivia and Emily.

Emily took his breath away.

Olivia had done the same thing, but she'd choked the breath from him.

Finished with breakfast, he headed back to the

stables, thinking about what the next few hours would bring and wishing Emily were here.

Donovan could be himself alongside Emily.

He thought about the two, with Olivia paling in comparison, and realized he was being unfair. Olivia had never misrepresented herself. She was Nolan Tate's daughter through and through. She knew what she wanted and how to get it. Stepping on people never bothered her. She kept her eye on the prize and ignored what was happening around her.

Emily knew what she wanted too. And her goals all centered around others. Not herself.

Donovan thought about last night and the whole family gathered in the hospital's waiting room. Olivia's older sister had gone into labor while Nolan was negotiating some prime real estate. Donovan had been sitting on his right and Olivia had texted him, wanting to know how long he and her father would be. She'd never even asked if he could come now instead of later when it was all over.

Donovan considered his debt to her father, who'd almost become his father-in-law. For the first time, Donovan truly understood why he'd broken up with Olivia and the relief he'd felt after it was all over.

Even though it put him in binding debt.

Debt was a lot easier to deal with than marrying for the wrong reasons.

Chapter Thirteen

Three hours of sleep was not enough. Emily parked her truck in the back of the museum, walked around to the front and unlocked the door. In college, she'd learned that it was always best to open a museum's door in plain sight because back doors didn't offer as much protection.

Stepping inside, she switched on the lights and took a deep breath. The place smelled slightly of wood, some recent visitor's perfume and aged things.

Until yesterday, it had been her favorite scent.

Today, her favorite scent was baby.

She locked the door behind her and quickly stashed her purse in the cabinet up front. Then walked up and down the aisles—she hadn't had time to finish yesterday—and made sure all was in place. The most valuable piece, pricewise, was a kachina believed to be over seven hundred years old. She didn't tell her visitors its worth. And she truly believed that if the museum's patrons had to guess the most valuable display, they'd easily skip over the aged kachina. Unlike some of its showy neighbors, all secured in stabilizing stands and behind glass, it was very simple, almost looking as if it was made on a flat piece of wood and drawn by a child. Its neighbors were all from the 1920s up to the 40s. Emily was constantly on the lookout to find one from the early 1900s—to be donated, of course. The museum's budget would not stretch to purchase.

Once she ascertained that all was right with her world, she checked her emails. After a dozen waste-of-her-time messages, she read one from a museum in Albuquerque. Its curator had visited the Heard Museum last week, studied the display on forgotten tribes and now wondered if Emily had anything else from the Salado that she'd be willing to lend. Reading between the lines, Emily could tell the woman wanted the tiny reddish bowl with faded black-and-white paint etched on the sides that Emily had lent to the Heard. And more if she had them. She had five more bowls and a few farming utensils.

Lending them out and providing their history not only promoted the Lost Dutchman Museum but allowed her to share the Salado with a whole generation who might not learn about them if not for her efforts.

Quickly, she searched the internet for the museum, as well as the name of the curator asking for the favor. Okay, the request wasn't coming from a huge museum, one she'd heard of, but it was coming from a facility that had been around more than sixty years. Good, she wouldn't need to worry about bankruptcy.

Another plus was the curator had included the date she wanted to open the exhibit, agreed to pay for shipping and had the date she'd return the objects.

Since the curator was aiming for August, Emily was inclined to consider the request. Of course, she'd need to put it before the board.

Skimming the Albuquerque museum's offerings, she looked for something she might ask for in exchange. She needed something to wow Apache Creek and encourage the locals it was time to visit again, something new to see.

When she figured out exactly what she needed, she sat back, feeling both exhilarated and skeptical. The museum in Albuquerque actually had a traveling dinosaur collection. The reviews from the schools in the state were stellar. Apparently, the replicas not only looked real, some built to scale, but even *moved*.

Not only that, but it was a hands-on exhibit.

The Lost Dutchman had no bones, none belonging to ancient Native Americans, lost miners or even their mules.

Right now, Emily wasn't too fond of bones. The last she'd seen had belonged to Billy Wilcox.

But, if she could bring the traveling dinosaur collection to Apache Creek, the animatronic replicas might not only put them in the black for months to come, but also allow her to purchase a few more much-needed displays.

She could expand.

Before she could formulate a return email, someone knocked at the front door. She looked at the time in the top right corner of her computer screen and jumped up. They'd officially been open for thirty minutes.

She quickly unlocked the door. Randall Tucker stood just outside.

"Are you open today? I heard the restaurant was closed last night…"

"We're open. I got busy and forgot to unlock the door." She stepped aside. The curator in her wanted to welcome him, but the naturalist wanted to slam the door in his face. The Christian in her said, "Are you here to visit the museum, or did you need to see me?"

"I'd like to see the museum."

He's just another person, she told herself as she took his payment and led him into the main room. Ten minutes later, a family of three—all senior citizens—had joined the tour, and she led them out of the museum and to the side.

Tucker jumped right in with the others when

they started asking questions. In just under an hour, they'd been introduced to Jacob Waltz, as well as the Salado, and even Native American artifacts on loan from her family.

Tucker mentioned the Naomi Humestewa connection, and she downplayed it. Later, he listened attentively to the byplay between her and the other visitors about the various gems, minerals and copper discovered in the area.

Between the museum and the barn was a replica of a shanty as well as two crumbling Conestoga wagons. It proved too hot for the seniors, who went back inside to purchase Lost Dutchman map souvenirs. Emily followed them to the gift shop and rang in their purchases. They nodded their thanks before heading to their vehicle.

"About how many visitors do you get a day?" Tucker asked when she rejoined him outside.

"It's the end of June and getting hot, so not many. We get more during the winter months. Why?"

"Just curious. I heard in town that you've some of the auctioned items from the Majestic. Mind if I see?"

"They're in the barn."

He followed her, admired the ancient sign and key cubbies and asked to see the ledger book. "My mom was an Elvis fan. Saw him in concert once."

Emily shrugged and led him back outside, moving toward the parking lot and where the cars were. She really wanted him to go.

"What are your plans for all this?" He didn't get the hint.

"I want to grow the museum."

"Inside looked pretty full. You plan to convert the barn? It has good bones."

There was that word again: *bones*.

"Maybe."

"Plans already made?" Tucker asked.

"No, right now it's just a dream." She didn't really like answering all his questions because she didn't trust him. It didn't matter that he'd appeared interested while touring the museum.

"I understand having dreams." He looked around. "How far back does the property go?"

"All the way to the base of the mountain."

Tucker whistled and finally got into his car, waving as he drove away as if he were a typical visitor.

He. Was. Not.

Two more visitors showed up. Emily showed them around and answered questions. They were more lookers than listeners and were ready to leave in under twenty minutes. They didn't buy any souvenirs.

Finally, she managed to sit down and shoot an email off to the museum's trustees as well as an "I'm interested" nod to the curator in Albuquerque.

By the time she closed down at four, she had a

meeting with the trustees scheduled for the day after tomorrow, Thursday evening, here in her office. She'd need to clean the table off. Tomorrow, between visitors, she'd put together a proposal. She'd wow them.

When she got to the Lost Dutchman Ranch, she hurried to her room and changed out of her khakis and into a pair of jeans. Looking around her room, for a brief moment she went back in time. This was the room of her childhood. Schoolbooks still cluttered the shelves amidst the mysteries and romances. Her Bible was open on the bedside table. She'd been reading Matthew, and now was seriously behind.

Her computer waited on a desk. Last time she'd used it, she'd been researching Kykotsmovi, Arizona, her mother's birthplace. Man, had she really been so busy these past few months that work on her manuscript had been forgotten? Snapping her jeans, she walked to the computer and looked at the notebook open beside it. Her uncles were mostly silversmiths. She'd been researching how far back.

She'd gotten so busy living in the present that she'd forgotten how much she loved the past.

Her phone pinged. She'd been getting messages all day, mostly from her dad and sister. She already knew that Eva loved breastfeeding, that her dad thought Naomi was going to be left-handed like her grandmother had been and that Naomi liked to sleep.

That seemed obvious and a silly thing to text, but Eva wasn't even a full day recovered from a twelve-hour labor. She could be forgiven.

Checking her texts, she read one from Eva: Jesse is not sharing when it comes to holding Naomi. Be ready to fight. Dad texted for Emily to make sure the sign saying the restaurant was closed went back up. Elise texted, The baby smiled at me!

No fair.

Quickly, Emily donned a new shirt and hurried out of her room, down the hallway, through the lobby and into the restaurant. The signs were up, but the restaurant wasn't empty.

Donovan stood where the game center was, watching the television and motioning for her to join him. Something about the way he stood worried her. She could hear the television now. He was watching the news. Something she never did because it depressed her.

"Emily, hurry."

She made her feet move quickly, stopping next to him and not protesting when he put his arm around her, his eyes still riveted to the screen.

"Age progression," she breathed, "on Billy Wilcox."

If not for a wealthy homeowner and a builder with a few minutes of time on his hands, Billy Wilcox would still be buried. Donovan wanted to look away from the television. This kid, because twenty-four was still a kid, had been buried where Donovan had worked. He looked at Emily, so sensitive, hurting even. What had she said about the skeleton, even before they knew who it was? *The skeleton belongs to somebody's son, brother, father, husband. We don't know. That means there's someone else out there who doesn't know.*

"I took a class," Emily said softly, "at Arizona State where an instructor had us read a case history about an eight-year-old girl taken from her Native American family in the 1920s. The girl went missing when she was ten. Eighty years later she was reunited with her family thanks to age-regression photos and DNA."

"Amazing." It was the only thing Donovan could think of to say.

"We looked at faces all the time in South Dakota. At first, I wasn't interested in forensics. But, after digging up all those bones, I wanted to see their faces, try to imagine their stories."

"Did you ever identify one of the skeletons you unearthed?"

"No, we registered them with the Native American Graves Protection and Repatriation Act, but there were too many and no reason. Unlike Billy, there was no murderer to bring to justice."

Someday he'd ask her to tell him more.

"What they've done with Billy's likeness is fascinating. On one hand," Emily said, "it would be easy for a forensic composition specialist to progress him agewise. His last school photo would have been at seventeen, so the shape and appearance of his face wouldn't change drastically."

"He looks a lot like Karl," Donovan observed. "A much younger Karl."

Emily stilled and then pulled out her cell phone. Soon Donovan heard her ordering Elise to "make sure Karl doesn't watch the news alone. He does not need to be caught by surprise watching his son age on television."

The conversation was quick, so Donovan assumed that Elise must have hurried into Karl's room. The news story changed from Billy to a weather report.

Donovan turned off the television and said, "I'm impressed with how quickly they got this progression done."

"Digital age," Emily mused, "but then there wouldn't be any digital photos. They'd have to use a print. I wonder if there's an archive somewhere that automatically keeps up with the likeness of missing children."

"Only for a brief time did the news show Billy as a child." Donovan had paid attention. "It mainly showed what Billy would have looked like when he died, about age twenty-four. His nose was bigger than it was in his school picture, and a little bit of a mustache shadowed above his top lip."

"I don't think Karl ever had facial hair."

"And," Donovan added, "they flashed a phone number three or four times, asking people to call if they recognized the young man."

"So they never said his name?" Emily asked.

"They didn't."

Emily walked from the room, turning off a few lights and checking the doors.

"You heading for the hospital?" Donovan asked.

"I am. Want to come?"

"No, there's a few things I need to do tonight. I'll be in Phoenix, though. If I finish early, I'll come by."

She shrugged, the casual kind of shrug that meant to relay little to no concern. Donovan knew, though, that she was curious. No way did he want to tell her he was having dinner with Randall Tucker.

The only reason Donovan wanted to meet in Phoenix was to get away from prying eyes. Since the Sunday lunch at the Miner's Lamp, he'd been expecting Emily to ask him about his meeting with Tucker and the blueprint the man had spread across the table.

Either Emily's friend Jane had been in the kitchen the whole time Tucker had been showing the blueprint—possible—or she hadn't had time to tell Emily—more likely.

This time, thanks to the news story, Donovan arrived five minutes late. Tucker had chosen an upscale restaurant, one where a sixty-dollar tab for a party of two was the norm. Thankfully, it was also one where you left feeling as though you wouldn't need to eat for a week.

Tuesday night wasn't busy. Tucker had snagged a corner booth. He already had a salad in front of him and was on his cell phone, but he motioned for Donovan to sit across from him.

Donovan did, picking up the menu and giving the man time to finish the call.

Apparently, Tucker had a daughter, one who exasperated him in ways only a female could manage. "I'd love for you to come to Apache Creek," Tucker said, "but there's nothing to do. Why don't you go stay with your aunt and uncle at the beach house? You've always loved doing that."

Then, Tucker spent a full minute nodding while he listened. Finally, he got to talk again.

"There's horseback riding and a museum. I think you could even go on a gold-panning expedition."

This time Donovan could hear the excited female tone.

"I'll book you a room and see you tomorrow." Ending the call, Tucker looked across at Donovan and said, "Well, that was unexpected. My daughter wants to come stay with me for a few weeks."

"You'll be in Apache Creek that long?"

"I purchased a home here back when I bought the Majestic. Then, I had some dealings in Maine.

I got back about two weeks ago. I intend to stay for a while."

"How old is your daughter?" Donovan knew that Tucker was older. But that didn't mean he didn't have a ten-year-old who now needed watching. The museum and gold panning were usually "just once" activities.

"She's twenty-one and about to be a senior in college. We go through this every summer. She finishes up a session of summer school, gets offered the beach or Europe, and chooses to come stay with me wherever I am."

"What about her mother?" Donovan asked before he really thought about how much he actually wanted to know about the man.

"She died when Betsy was four. I hired a nanny, one who could travel, and up until Betsy was in high school, she lived in thirteen different states while I worked."

"What happened in high school?"

"I asked her where her favorite place we'd lived was. She said San Diego. We moved there, she went to school and I took a much-needed break."

It was a side to Tucker Donovan hadn't found during his internet research. The true test, of course, would be when Donovan met the daughter. Would she be like Olivia or would she be like Emily?

Donovan ordered. For a while, the two men talked about Apache Creek and the Superstition

Mountains. Then, once the waitress cleared their table, Tucker took a blueprint from the seat beside him.

"These are just preliminary sketches. I've indicated where homes could go. I've also allotted more square feet per home. I think if you were willing to design each home so it blended with the background of the Superstitions, we could raise the asking price and make even more than if we simply did a development with multiple, similar houses."

"When were you thinking of going forward with this project?"

"In the next month."

Donovan shook his head. "Karl just received devastating news. I'm not willing to add to his distress. He might agree to sell to you now, but I'm not sure he wouldn't later come to regret it."

"I agree," Tucker said, surprising Donovan. "I intend to find another half parcel. I'll limit the number of houses to eight an acre, unless you have something else to suggest." He tapped on the blueprint.

Sure enough, a half parcel had been loosely designed.

"And this is going to be a retirement community?"

"Yes. You'll see that I've paid attention to—"

"Apache Creek doesn't have a hospital."

Tucker nodded. "Yet, each winter over a thousand snowbirds occupy the RV parks. The lack of a hospital hasn't deterred seniors from making this a part-time home."

"Your development might not cater to snowbirds."

"True. Phoenix is next door. It's not that much of a drive. How far did you have to drive to the hospital when you were growing up in Mytal, Nebraska?"

The hospital was down the road from the high school, over an hour away.

"You've spent some time researching me," Donovan said.

"And I liked everything I found. I like even more what I've personally watched. Instead of sulking when the Baer job came to a halt and old Tate didn't send you anywhere else, you immediately got a job on your own. And, if I'm not mistaken, it's not the job or the Superstition Mountains that draw you to this area."

Donovan wanted to say that nothing drew him to an area. He wasn't the kind of guy who wanted to stay anywhere. There was too much to see. He'd have loved following his family to thirteen different locations while growing up.

"Emily Hubrecht is a lovely young lady."

"Emily doesn't think much of you," Donovan said honestly.

"No, she doesn't. But first impressions can change. Look, you left our meeting on Sunday giving me an 'I'll think about it.' We're talking a job that might take up to five years because I'll probably buy another parcel. That's how much I believe in this area." Tucker handed over the blueprint. "Take it, look at it, play with it, make it your own. This meeting today, well, I'm hoping I've given you more to think about."

Five years near Emily, without his job affecting Karl or the land on Ancient Trails Road?

Donovan didn't hesitate this time. "I'm definitely interested."

Chapter Fourteen

Emily knew the exact moment Donovan entered Eva's hospital room. It was as if the air changed, got fuller, more buoyant. She made herself more comfortable in the faux-leather green chair and tried to act nonchalant as he made his way to her side.

"I finished my meeting early," he said.

"Baer going to start building again?" Jacob asked.

"I'm not sure, but I'll tell you the minute I know."

Emily refused to let that declaration ruin the mood she was in. "Come look." She led Donovan over to a tiny crib where Naomi, oblivious to her surroundings, lay sleeping. "Eva says we can't hold her for another hour."

"She needs to sleep without being held or we'll be holding her for the next three years," Eva protested.

"I volunteer," said Jacob.

Emily thought she'd never been more in love with her own father. "Were you like this with us?"

"Yes, he was," Eva said. "I remember when you were born. I was a little older than Timmy. Mom was always telling him to let you sleep in the crib. She kept telling me the same thing, too. I'm going to grab one of the nurses and see if I can't talk her into letting Timmy see Naomi. There has to be a way. We'll stand behind glass or something. You," she said to Emily, "had no rules concerning respiratory viruses. I think they even let Elise hold you, and she picked her nose!"

"I did not!"

"You were a beautiful baby," Jacob said to Emily.

"You probably said that about all your daughters." Jilly tucked a corner of the baby's blanket so it more firmly cocooned her.

"You have children?" Emily asked. Sometimes she forgot that it had only been a year since Jilly purchased the old house just a mile from the ranch. Plus, these past few days she'd been so focused on the baby, on the museum and on Donovan, that figuring out what was going on between her father and Jilly had been more or less second thought.

"Some fool nurse," Jacob said, "tried to instruct me on proper infant holding."

"My husband died just a few months after we

married. I've—" she smiled Jacob's way "—not found anyone to compare in a long, long time."

There were no places to sit. When Emily moved from her chair, Elise snagged it.

"Where's Cooper?" Donovan asked.

"Down with Karl," Eva answered. "Timmy's there, too."

"I'm glad you saw the news," Elise said. "I hurried to his room and changed the channel. He's grumbling about not getting to see it, but I told him he needs cheering up."

"What is he watching?" Jilly asked.

"*Scooby Doo* with Timmy."

"We could go down there and visit," Emily offered. "Karl's awake. He'll get out tomorrow."

"I'd like that," Donovan said.

"We're taking him to stay with us. He'll sleep in Eva's old room."

"Please," Eva urged her dad, "call it the guest room. I'm not moving back."

Jacob sat up straight. "No, when Karl gets better and returns home, I'm turning it into a children's room. Naomi will spend the night often because I'll put in a crib. And then when you have little Jacob…"

"Hmmph." Jesse lifted his head and turned to face his father-in-law. "We're not promising to name the next one Jacob."

"Next one?" Eva said.

Elise spoke up, "Cooper and I will name a son after you, Dad."

"There will be nothing left for me," Emily protested.

"Better get her downstairs and visiting Karl," Jesse advised Donovan. "Once this family starts planning, you just might find yourself part of the plan whether you want it or not."

Eva proved that she'd not forgotten the pillow-throwing wars from childhood. Jesse merely took the extra pillow, stuffed it under his head and closed his eyes.

Elise wound up accompanying them. Karl's room wasn't as crowded. Timmy sat on the bed playing checkers with Karl. Garrett slouched in a chair texting on his phone.

"Girlfriend," Cooper mouthed from the other chair, where he'd been reading a magazine but now stood to give Elise the seat. He shot a look at Garrett, who immediately stood for Emily's benefit.

Cooper and Elise exchanged a look.

"Timmy, are you guys about done with the game?"

"Oh," Karl said, "I beat him soundly a good five minutes ago. We're just practicing moves now."

Elise sat on the edge of the bed. Cooper motioned for Garrett to end the texting.

"Karl, there's no way to avoid this. You'll be

watching the news sometime this week and they'll probably show some photos of Billy."

"I know," Karl said sadly. "They were on earlier today. He looked a lot like me."

Elise and Cooper exchanged looks Emily interpreted as *all that worry for nothing*.

"You're all right, then?"

"It was just the shock the first time. I just wasn't expecting it. I guess I thought I'd never know. And to think, he was twenty-four and trying to come home. I hope they find whoever did this."

Elise took his hand. "Me, too, Karl."

"Let's pray," Cooper suggested.

Emily noted that Donovan looked a little surprised when she reached for one of his hands and Garrett reached for the other. But he bowed his head and seemed to listen intently as Cooper prayed for everyone involved, including whoever had buried Billy Wilcox.

"You hungry?" Emily asked Donovan after the prayer.

"I could eat."

"Good." Emily didn't invite anyone else. It seemed sometimes as if she and Donovan were rarely alone. She wanted to be. If this thing with Karl and Billy was solved, her life would be back to perfect.

The hospital cafeteria was closed to a hot-meal option. There was, however, a convenience section. Emily chose bottled water, a packet of cookies, plus a salad and packet of ranch dressing.

"You didn't take anything?" she accused. "You were hungry."

"Maybe I was hungry for good company."

She ate in silence, just enjoying his presence across from her. Others came in and sat at the tables nearby. Some were families with fear on their faces; others had joy. Now and then a single person came and sat. The doctors and nurses always seemed in a hurry.

"I like your family," Donovan said when she'd finished the last bite.

"I like them, too."

"I can see why you don't want to work anywhere else."

"I had a job offer a week ago," she shared. "It was perfect. It was for the Native American Heritage Museum. I wouldn't be curator, but I'd be an assistant."

"You turned it down," he guessed.

"Without hesitation. You saw my family. Not a chance do I want to live three states away next time Eva has a baby."

"What if the person you loved lived three states away? I mean, would Eva follow Jesse if he asked her to?"

"You need to ask Jesse about his family. You'd need a crowbar to get him to move."

"And that's probably a good analogy for you,

a crowbar to get you to move even if you fall in love with someone who couldn't live in Apache Creek."

"There's a difference between couldn't and wouldn't," Emily said. "It would depend a lot on who is giving up what and why."

Donovan wanted to think he could live in Apache Creek forever. What he couldn't share with Emily, though he wanted to, was that thinking about staying here for just five years felt restricting.

Yet he was absolutely willing to do it for her. He'd just like the reassurance that if an opportunity of a lifetime arose for him, she'd be willing to compromise.

But she owed him nothing and maybe didn't have a clue how much he liked her.

"You know," he said, "this past week has been pretty amazing."

"Amazing," she agreed.

"I'm just wondering if, maybe, you'd like to go out on a date, a real date. Dinner and a movie. This Friday?"

She opened her bag of cookies, divided them evenly between them and said, "I think I'd like that."

He took a cookie, bit into it and said, "Chocolate chip, my favorite."

"I didn't know that. In fact, there's a lot about

you I don't know. It's really not fair. You know everything about me."

He wasn't ready to tell her about the debt he owed to Olivia's father. Though, if he and Emily did go out a few more times, he'd need to tell her. Tucker's offer sounded good, but Donovan couldn't chance not paying Nolan Tate off.

"What do you want to know?" He hoped she'd ask something easy.

"Tell me more about your parents. I know you grew up on a dairy farm and never go back. Did you have any brothers or sisters? Why did you leave?"

"I left because I felt stifled. Except for school and an occasional night in town, my world began and ended on the farm. My mom and dad loved me, but there was just the three of us. They'd both been only children, too. My mom was in her early forties when I was born, so I had no grandparents or cousins or siblings."

She smiled. "Just wait until you meet my family in the Kykotsmovi Village. I've known them forever but there are so many, I sometimes say the wrong name."

"Your family is like a whole different world to me."

"Tell me about your dad," she suggested.

He thought back to all the years he'd worked alongside his dad to keep the farm going. He remembered early mornings when he'd bring the cows into the holding area and guide them to the right stall. Next, he helped with prepping the udder before putting the milkers on. His dad had often reminisced about when he did the milking by hand. The only thing Donovan remembered was attaching the metal pipes to the teats, over and over, one cow to the next, in an assembly line.

"My dad listened to classical music while we milked the cows."

"That's a start," Emily encouraged.

Olivia had once asked about his family, but within minutes he'd lost her.

"At the peak of my father's career, we had almost a thousand Holsteins, and we employed five. The most important time of day is morning milking, followed by afternoon milking."

To Donovan's surprise, Emily listened intently, interrupting only twice to question him. She liked that he called the cows "girls" and scolded him for appreciating school only because it meant he didn't have to help with the cleanup after morning milking.

"How many Holsteins does your dad have now?"

"I think—" it pained him to admit he wasn't sure "—that he's down to about forty-two."

Now, Donovan sent money to his parents so they could pay someone to work the farm. The first check he'd sent six years ago came back inside a folded piece of notebook paper with the words, scrawled by his father's hand, "The farm has been in the family for almost seventy years and was meant for you to work it." His mother, however, had sent a note thanking him for thinking of them, telling him how the tomato plants were doing and sharing a few stories about one of the new calves.

Four years ago, Donovan's dad, Raymond Russell, stopped returning the checks and cashed them. Plus, his handwritten scrawls turned to "Call your mother once in a while."

Two years ago, engaged to Olivia, Donovan had been sending quite a bit. Now, not so much. His debt to Nolan Tate interfered.

"What does the farm look like?"

That he could answer without feeling like a heel. He loved the home he'd grown up in. "My family's only the second owner of a 1906 structure with a double winged-gable roof and original hardwood floors. It has personality. Some of my favorite moments growing up involved working alongside my dad doing restoration. Only, he called it repairs."

And with that the good memories tumbled forward. "I was itching to ride the hay wagon with your dad this past Saturday. I used to love to ride ours during baling." Emily didn't seem too impressed with that one, but her eyes lit up when he talked about sledding.

"Problem was," he ended, "I did all those things

alone. When I went off to college, I think my biggest dream was to never be alone again."

"But you travel from place to place alone and live in a small camper alone."

"Yes, but until recently, it didn't feel lonely."

Looking around the cabin the next morning, Donovan came to the conclusion that he was already moved in. Clothes were strewed across chairs. Tucker's blueprints were on the kitchen table. All his electronics, phone and iPad were plugged in. Change, gum wrappers, keys and a few paper clips were on the nightstand.

Today he needed to work on Tinytown. He had quite a few ideas, already expanding from the quick outline he'd shared with Jacob more than a week ago.

If—and it was a really big if—he decided to work for Randall Tucker, he needed to figure in time to work on Tinytown, or Timmy and Emily might never forgive him.

Sitting at the table, he turned Tucker's blueprints over. He'd not be using them. If the man did hire him, Donovan had his own ideas about what a community here should look like. Quickly, he arranged Tinytown, thinking about what would make Timmy happy and what extras would be affordable and unique. Before Donovan knew it, he was in danger of missing breakfast. He rolled the blueprint up, tucked it under his arm and took a slow, meandering walk to the dining room.

So much potential.

He filled his plate before he sat down. Emily waved at him from across the room, where she was giving advice to a couple he'd not seen before. They must have arrived yesterday. Then, she came over and handed him a big glass of milk before he even ordered it.

"I head off to work after I finish serving breakfast. I'll be back about four thirty. Tonight's church. Why don't you come with me?"

A million reasons why he shouldn't went through his head. Followed by a single thought of why he should.

Emily invited him.

"I'll think about it."

"That's a better answer than last time I asked."

Timmy came in, sat down next to him and nodded at the blueprints. "Can I see?"

Emily brought over a glass of milk for Timmy and said, "Get breakfast first. When you're done, Grandpa says he needs some help down at the barn."

Timmy sighed. "I wish Dad would come home. Grandpa keeps putting me to work. I never get to play video games except at night when I'm in Karl's room."

"Karl getting out today?" Donovan asked.

Emily collected his now-empty plate. "Garrett's going to get him this afternoon."

"When will Eva come home?"

"Tomorrow. Jesse's bringing her, and Grandpa's been ordered to stay home."

Timmy fetched a plate of eggs, sausage and ketchup. "Good man." Together Timmy and Donovan high-fived.

While Timmy ate, Donovan spread out the blueprint and discussed his ideas. "When we sat with your grandpa, we decided not just houses."

"I remember."

"So, this morning while I walked from my cabin to here, I detoured and looked at the area where we might build this."

"Not by the schoolhouse where we do crafts," Timmy advised.

"Why not?"

"Because then when it's time to do crafts," Timmy said in a loud whisper, "whoever the teacher is can just call us. We need to be farther away."

"I was thinking next to the pool."

Timmy frowned. "That would be better than the tennis court. I wouldn't want to get hit by any balls."

"Anyone use the tennis court?" Donovan thought it looked fairly run-down.

"Not that I've seen."

"If we put it by the pool, parents can watch their

children." Quickly Donovan showed were he'd put the fire station, store and hospital.

"The hospital should have two beds," Timmy advised. "One for sick people and one for mommies who are having babies."

Donovan wasn't about to touch that topic. "And, we'll put the movie theater here, but we'll make it a drive-in. I think you can talk your grandpa into finding a bunch of old pedal cars. We'll restore them, and then you can sit in them and watch movies at night."

"Awesome."

"Houses will be here and there." He pointed to the spots.

Before Donovan could react, Timmy removed a red crayon from his pocket and added a house to the left of the movie theater.

"Good."

Emily came back, scooted Timmy out the door, and then before Donovan had a chance to make small talk, she'd cleaned the last table and headed back to the main house.

He'd never been inside. Didn't know what their living space looked like. All he knew was Elise was getting ready to marry Cooper and move a few miles down the road. Eva's house was close by, still on Lost Dutchman Ranch property, and only Jacob and Emily still really called the place home.

Home.

Donovan rolled the blueprint up and headed for the door. He had something to do, something he should have done long ago.

It was time to strengthen the bond that was home. He'd ignored the pull of his family's love, intent on proving himself. Now he realized that proving himself was empty if his parents weren't part of the plan.

His mom picked up on the second ring. Her first words, after hearing his voice, were "What's wrong?"

"Nothing, Mom. I just wanted to call."

Silence.

He tried to imagine Emily calling Jacob and having nothing to talk about. Wouldn't happen. For one thing, they texted each other about six times a day—twenty right now, but that had to do with the new baby.

"I just thought I'd catch you up on my life and find out what you're doing. I miss you."

Silence again, only this time he heard her sniffling and realized she was crying, silently.

"Son." His dad took the phone. "What's wrong?"

Great, his parents both thought that the only reason he'd be calling them out of the blue was if something was wrong.

"Dad, I've met a girl."

To Donovan's amazement, his dad stayed on the line while his mother got on the other line. At the end, after Donovan had shared everything from the petitions, to the skeleton, to the fact that he was now renting a cabin from the family, and even Emily's invitation to church tonight, his dad said, "Maybe this one you could bring *home* to meet us?"

"I have to win her first," Donovan said. "Right now we're just friends."

But he didn't want to be, and he didn't want to wait until their date on Friday night to wow her.

Chapter Fifteen

The museum had had ten visitors this morning. All at once. They'd oohed and aahed and walked around. One was a movie buff, and Emily had taken him to see what she had left from the Majestic.

Funny, she didn't see the Majestic as history, not like the Native American artifacts that her family had donated, but it was part of the personal history for many visitors.

"I stayed there in 1963," the man shared. "I remember meeting a movie star in the dining room. I was so thrilled. I remember telling him he was my favorite."

"Who was it?"

"Wish I remembered." After they exited the barn, the man left a hundred-dollar bill in the donation box.

At noon, the last visitor cleared out. Emily

checked her emails and fetched the lunch Cook had packed for her. Another perk of living at home.

She'd just taken her first bite when the door opened. She brushed away crumbs that might not be there and hurried to the front desk. Donovan entered the room.

"I," he announced, "just had the best idea."

Without waiting for her response, he looked around the front foyer and then went behind the counter and into her office. She followed, protesting, "It's a mess in here."

She'd not met a curator who kept a neat office. She had boxes waiting to be filled, inventory waiting to be restocked, as well as a dozen huge books turned to various pages all with vital information about the artifacts in her museum.

He carefully scooted some of the boxes on her worktable aside and laid down a blueprint. It wasn't like any blueprint she'd seen.

"I worked on this all morning. It was in my mind, and then because Cook asked me to watch the dining room while he took a break—"

"Where's Elise?" Emily interrupted.

"She went into Phoenix to visit Eva."

"Oh, she's getting to see Naomi more than me." Emily checked her watch. She had six hours to go before she could head for the hospital.

Donovan continued, "I wound up watching Timmy, too. I guess your dad's on the internet ordering a few things that the baby might need."

Time to pull dad's credit card.

"So, now that I know the Hubrecht clan better, I revised my plans a bit."

He spread the blueprint out, using a giant book to hold one end and an old hammer for the other. He'd added a whole section to the Tinytown she remembered from his first attempt. He won points, too, because some of the drawings were done by Timmy's hand.

"You're getting more excited," she mentioned. She'd seen him this way before, talking about Karl having an underground home and then, too, when he described the tree houses he'd designed.

"I thought I was done," Donovan said, "when I designed the drive-in movie theater complete with cars, but then... I mentioned this to your father, but wanted to run it by you. He didn't say anything, but I could tell he had misgivings."

"What about?" She started getting excited, too.

"Instead of just making this small-town America, why don't we also do a Native American section, the Hopi section, in honor of your family?"

"You'd do that?" she queried. "For me?"

She looked up, her eyes big, and Donovan realized he'd do just about anything she asked, just to keep those eyes so focused. Yup, he was in trouble.

Take the job. Stay.

"That's an awesome idea," she said, oblivious

to his thoughts, "but it doesn't belong at the Lost Dutchman Ranch."

"Where does it belong?"

"Here, at my museum. And if you were going to do it, it would take money and time. But, just think of what you could create. The Hopis lived in pueblos made of dried clay and stone. You ever work with that?" While she spoke, she thought about the cost. Then, she thought about the museum in Albuquerque.

He managed not to roll his eyes. He'd built a home in Santa Fe, New Mexico, year before last. Now, if ever there was a city that demanded authenticity, it was Santa Fe.

Her eyes crinkled. He might not have rolled his eyes, but she already—apparently—knew him well enough to know he wanted to.

"Don't think you're so smart," she warned. "It's not just a single structure. My ancestors occupied what you might consider an apartment building with multiple living areas so that whole families lived together."

"Not tepees?" This was more than he'd expected, and he fervently wished he'd researched what he was offering before he offered it. Now, he wouldn't be able to step away from the sight of those big eyes looking at him while her voice complimented him on his awesome idea.

"We don't have to build to scale," he cautioned.

She wrinkled her nose. "For the ranch, maybe

I have another idea. And I know we don't have to build to scale." She hesitated. "Maybe instead of a Hopi section, maybe you could build a hotel."

"What?"

"You could build me a child-size replica of the Majestic."

"You're kidding?"

"No, and it would be just the type of cross advertising that could save the museum. Along with the dinosaurs."

Okay, she was expecting too much. "I don't do dinosaurs."

She laughed, standing next to him, leaning in to him, so close he could smell her perfume. It was too much. He touched her shoulder, and she stopped talking about some museum in New Mexico that had a traveling dinosaur museum and looked at him.

For a moment, he couldn't breathe.

"I can't wait until Friday night," he said.

"Me, either. We'll have a good time."

"No," he said, "I mean, I can't wait until Friday night."

Then, he kissed her.

Donovan left the blueprints with Emily. She'd helped with building plans before. Good thing he might be here for five years. Tinytown would soon be anything but tiny. Heading back to the Lost Dutchman, he grabbed a boxed lunch and said goodbye to Jacob, who was on his way to the hospital. Then he settled on the porch of his cabin in his favorite rocking chair, called Randall Tucker but got his voice mail and then spent the rest of the day putting together a cost analysis for the first phase of Tinytown.

Jacob came home a little while later.

No matter what Emily wanted, he'd start with the easy buildings first.

Elise drove up, parked right in front of the entrance to the ranch, ran around the car and helped Karl inside. Donovan would have helped, but the woman was fast. She had him inside before Donovan could even make it to the bottom of his cabin's stairs.

He went back to planning. By building one new section or building each year, children could be playing and looking forward to the new additions next time.

Cooper drove up, parked by the barn and walked to the house. A moment later, Jilly arrived carrying a casserole dish. It made Donovan smile. That's what church people did when someone got out of the hospital. They brought food. Of course, most people didn't recuperate at a dude ranch with its own dining room.

He went back to planning, but the next vehicle got his full attention.

The squad car pulling in and parking by the barn pulled Donovan from his work. Police officer Sam Miller got out and walked toward the main house.

Quickly, Donovan texted Emily. Cop just came. Whole family here. What's happening?

Really? Sam's there?

How she knew it was Sam, he didn't know.

Sam's here in uniform.

Why?

Not sure. I was hoping you'd tell me.

I just closed. B right there.

He glanced at his watch. It was after four. He'd worked steadily for over three hours. After pushing himself up, he walked to the main house. It was quiet. Cook wasn't in the dining room's kitchen. A note on the door said it would reopen for dinner on Friday. The front desk was empty. It, too, had a sign directing him to ring a bell.

He rang. A minute later, Jacob came to the front and said, "I should have called you. Come on back. You'll want to hear this, too. It's about Billy."

Jacob didn't seem too worried. Donovan had no business interfering in what might be a private family matter—not that he believed for a moment that Jacob had done anything wrong—but Donovan had been involved since the moment he'd unearthed the yellowish-brown shards that had turned out to be Billy Wilcox.

Jacob led him into the living room. It was clearly a man's room, and Donovan wouldn't have changed one thing about it—not the lines, not the view, not the atmosphere. A couch was against one wall with two big leather recliners flanking it. A large plaque was on the wall stating As For Me and My House, We Shall Serve the Lord. Sam was in one of the chairs. Elise and Jilly were on the couch.

When did they all get here?

An oversize coffee table was in front of the couch. The television was huge, taking up half of one wall; the other half belonged to a fireplace. On the mantel were two wooden, obviously Native American, dolls. A grandfather clock as well as shelves of trophies and books occupied the third wall. The final wall had a *Star Wars* poster with Darth Vader looking down at a kid's train table and boxes of Legos scattered around. Obviously Timmy's domain.

"I texted Emily when I saw Sam get here," Donovan said, taking the other chair since it didn't look as though Jacob wanted to sit.

Jacob nodded. "Good thinking."

"I'm here." Emily all but skidded into the room. "What's happening?"

"News about Billy," Elise said before turning to Sam and saying, "Go on."

"We had over a dozen calls about the photos of Billy Wilcox. Three turned out viable."

"What happened to my son?" Karl asked.

Emily again sat on the armrest of the chair Donovan occupied. He reached over to pat her hand to let her know he cared, but instead she took his hand, curling her fingers between his, not letting go.

Sam leaned forward. "It's both good and bad, Karl. I'm not going to lie. We had a call from a woman who lives in Kearny, Arizona."

"I know the place," Karl said.

The front door opened and a moment later someone rang the bell. Elise said, "I'll get it."

Sam waited a moment before going on. "Billy worked for her from the time he was twenty up until he was about twenty-two."

"Doing what?"

Donovan admired that the others—all powerful personalities—let Karl do the asking.

"It was a small farm. Apparently he worked mostly for room and board. She says he never gave her any trouble, but he disappeared after about two years without saying goodbye."

"You sure it was Billy?"

"She faxed us a photo. I'll make sure you get a copy."

"Appreciate that."

"Here's where it gets a little sketchy. The other call that we believe accurate was from Irving Taylor."

"Never heard of him," Karl said.

"I have." Jacob looked out the big picture window at the panoramic view of cacti, desert and sand hills. "He has a ramshackle house, falling apart, just a few miles north of Ancient Trails Road."

"The one that's wood, stone and mud?" Cooper asked. "I didn't realize anyone lived there."

"Me, either," Elise said returning. To her dad, she said, "I just rented out the cabin next to Donovan's."

"Good."

"Irving won't answer the door to most people," Sam continued. "He probably hasn't spoken to anyone, really, in decades. I went out there today."

"He doesn't have electricity or plumbing. It's like going back in time a hundred years."

"You've been there, Dad?" Emily asked.

"Church has helped him out once or twice."

"I thought there was a law about plumbing?" Elise said.

"He contacted me," Sam said, bringing the conversation back on topic. "He was listening to a police scanner, of all things, and heard Billy Wilcox's name."

Karl sat up.

"He says Billy showed up about thirty years ago, skin and bones. Irving said he fed the boy and pointed him toward town. He said the kid acted lost."

The front door opened again. This time the bell didn't sound. Donovan figured it must be Jesse or someone who worked at the Lost Dutchman.

"How could he remember that long ago?" Donovan said.

Jacob answered, "When you don't get many visitors, you remember the ones you have."

Karl shook his head. "Billy knew that area. He wouldn't be lost."

"But," Emily reminded Karl, "the medical examiner said the bones showed signs of arthritis. There could be a wealth of struggles Billy dealt with."

Cooper put in, "The inability to walk, fatigue, muscle aches."

"His mother had arthritis," Emily told Donovan.

"In '83, when he would have been twenty-four, we didn't have cell phones or such to call for help. Back then, Ancient Trails Road wasn't a road. It was miles from a road. Naomi and I got turned around on our horses once. Rode for hours. I remember thanking God that we had water."

"You're not closing the case, are you?" Karl asked. "Because there is that knife, and it wasn't Billy's."

"No," Sam said. "We'll keep the file open for a while longer. But, thanks to the third phone call, we know who the knife belonged to."

"Who?"

Donovan couldn't say who asked the question first or if everyone asked at the same time. Didn't matter, because what mattered was who answered.

Patti de la Rosa stood in the doorway.

"It was mine."

Chapter Sixteen

No one had to urge Patti to keep on talking.

"I didn't put it together, didn't remember until I saw Billy's photograph on the television yesterday. I pulled out some of my scrapbooks this morning."

"Remember what?" Karl was starting to get cranky.

"What I won in that rodeo," Patti said to Jacob. "Do you remember?"

"No."

"I'm not surprised. You only had eyes for Naomi. And Billy Wilcox only had eyes for her, too. Me, I loved Billy, but I couldn't tell him. I was way too shy back then."

Her knees started to sway. Donovan was out of his chair and over to her side just in time to catch her. Emily was there, too, helping him, moving her to the chair while Elise ran for water.

Karl didn't look like he could move. "I'm not understanding all this," he said.

"I won the barrel racing event that day," Patti said. "I won all three runs. And, like all the other winners, I received a knife."

"Like Dad's."

"Exactly like your father's."

"But the initials aren't yours," Emily protested.

"Yes, they are. My first name is Jane. It's my middle name that is Patricia. Like I told you at the hospital, my mother was Jane, and we didn't like getting confused."

"And your maiden name was Hamm," Donovan said. "You told us the Gramma Hamm story."

"So, how did Billy get your knife?" Jacob wanted to know.

"I gave it to him. It was the next Monday at school. He said something about liking the way I rode. And, I gave it to him. I'd forgotten. How could I have forgotten?"

"So, probably not a murder weapon," Jacob said.

"Probably not," Officer Sam Miller said, standing. "I called the woman in Kearny back, and she remembered Billy having the knife. Most likely—" Sam went over to Karl and bent down, looking the old man in the eyes "—Billy was trying to get home and just too sick to make it all the way."

"I'd have fetched him if he called."

"We didn't find any money, nothing," Sam said.

"But you think he was trying to make it home?" Karl asked.

"I absolutely think that."

Karl nodded.

"Come on, Karl," Elise said. "This is way more excitement than you need on the day you get out of the hospital. I'm taking you to Eva's room. Cooper, you want to help?"

He was already out of his seat and at her side. Looking at the way they smiled at each other did something to Emily's insides. She wanted the same.

Her dad was walking both Sam and Patti to the door. Going over to stand by Donovan, Emily said, "Not the way I thought this would all pan out."

"Me, either," Donovan said, but Emily got the idea he wasn't talking about Billy Wilcox.

He was talking about her.

About them.

Donovan met the family in the dining room for dinner. It was still closed, for grandfather purposes, but Cook had made a meat loaf for the family.

To Donovan's surprise, Karl was there, dressed for church.

"Looks like you're coming tonight, too," Jacob observed.

"Yeah, well, Emily invited me."

"She know the answer was yes?" Cook asked, handing Donovan a plate.

"No."

"How long has it been since you've been to church?" Jacob queried.

"Too long."

Jacob nodded. "You picked the right night. The congregation will be so focused on Patti, they might actually miss noticing you."

"I doubt it," Karl said.

Emily came in at that moment, wearing a white shirt, tucked and nipped in all the right places, over a blue jean skirt and white sandals. Her hair was long and loose with some kind of band holding it back.

Donovan stood so quickly that the table moved.

"Easy, boy," Jacob cautioned.

Emily got her own plate and came to join them, completely at ease at the table full of men.

He should have attended church on Sunday morning, Donovan considered, because then he would have enjoyed this smile more than once.

Dinner ended too soon as they were already running late. Pleased that she didn't question who she'd be riding with, Donovan led the way to his truck, opened the passenger door and helped her in. Across the way, Jacob was doing the same, only he was helping Karl. Cook climbed in the back. Only Harold Mull stayed behind, to mind the animals and in case of an emergency. Donovan had been informed that usually emergencies weren't a consideration and everyone went, but with Eva in the hospital...

"I'm surprised Karl's attending church. He got out of the hospital today, and then he found out that his son died trying to get to him."

"He's not missed a day of church in the last year." Emily tugged on her seat belt. "It's his favorite thing."

Donovan wondered how long it would take him to convince her to sit in the middle, next to him, instead of by the window.

"You think my father has a female following," Emily added. "You should see the women flock about Karl. They take care of him. Tonight, he'll know he's not alone. Of course, he knows the Lord. Karl knows he's not alone."

Donovan shook his head. "I was sure that skeleton was a murder victim. What are the odds, that knife being right there?"

"I guess we humans are geared to think the worst."

"You certainly used to think the worst of me," he teased.

"Used to? Maybe I still do."

"No, you don't."

"You're right. Any man that starts out thinking he can win my affections by building me a Hopi village—"

"And then gets talked into a whole hotel—"

"—can't be all bad," she finished.

Donovan followed Jacob from the ranch, his truck bumping on the dirt road before finding traction. "I've got something to tell you," he said once they were on smoother pavement.

"About Tinytown?"

"No."

"About the Baer house?"

"No."

She started to guess again, but he held up his hand. "Randall Tucker's made me a job offer. He assures me it won't be Karl's or the Baer place. He's wanting to put in a retirement community, and he doesn't want it to be cookie-cutter. It's a five-year project. I'd be in charge. I'd be here."

"Tract housing?"

"Yes, and no. He's allowing multi-acre lots, and he wants diversity. So consider it a planned development but so much more."

"I don't like it."

Donovan wished he could tell her something that would make the scenario perfect, but this was his job. She had to understand. "It's coming whether I'm in charge or not."

"Can't you just build tree houses and—"

"I'd be moving from one state to the other, and when the economy tanks, I'm no longer worthy. Plus, the tree houses I build are for the wealthy. Tucker's already dangled the 'affordable' card in front of me."

And in the hours since he'd talked to his parents and spoken with Tucker, all Donovan could think about—besides Emily—was that maybe he could get his parents to move here. Retire. No more snow.

"Randall purchased the Majestic and didn't even try to build something modern but equivalent. He built an ordinary apartment building."

The way she emphasized the word *ordinary* let him know how deeply she still felt.

"I think he regrets his choice. Did you know he's purchased a house here in Apache Creek?"

"Where?"

"I don't know. He's going to make this his home base."

"He actually approached Karl," she said indignantly, "and his property wasn't for sale."

"Not an unheard-of or unexpected move in real estate."

"We're not Phoenix," she protested, but he could tell she was halfhearted.

"Better the enemy you know than the enemy you don't." Donovan couldn't believe he was using the exact same words on her that he'd wanted to use on Tucker. Of course, Donovan's nemesis was Nolan Tate. His ex-fiancée's dad. In this case, Emily might consider Donovan the enemy more than Tucker.

After a moment, Emily allowed, "Dad says

Apache Creek's had a good run, and that change is bound to come."

"Five years," Donovan said. "I'll be here five years. I called him this afternoon and took the job. I'm thinking that maybe after our first date this Friday night, there will be another?"

She nodded. "And then another."

He watched her relax and promised himself he wouldn't do anything that might cause her to exit his truck and not climb in again. Ever.

When he pulled into the parking lot of the Apache Creek Church, he saw only one carload of people he didn't recognize.

"Those are the Cagnalias," Emily said. "The boy walking beside his mother is Garrett's best friend."

Parking, Donovan managed to wave at John Westerfield and his family. "Guess I'll be able to hire him back."

Emily nodded and said, "There's always a positive."

"Who's the minister?"

"Mike Hamm. He's a little older than Eva—"

Donovan held up a hand. "You can give me the whole history later. Right now, I'm satisfied that I know his great-grandmother's history."

Church started with an assembly. He came to find out there were a few other people he didn't know in Apache Creek. He shook a dozen hands and tried to remember names. After the devotional, Emily dragged him to the singles class, and he found himself between her and Sam Miller.

Funny, he'd not thought of the man as being single. Elise and Cooper were in the class, although he figured they'd be booted in a few months when they got married.

Now he'd be here for the event.

Jane de la Rosa came into the classroom, a little late, and sat down next to Emily. She leaned in and whispered something. All Donovan could make out was "side of my mother I never knew about."

Too soon it was over, leaving Donovan glad he'd come and sorry to leave. It was a piece of his youth he'd missed. It had been one more thing caught up in his battle to get away from the farm.

The only place his father had never forsaken was church. But they always went home right after, just in case the cows needed attention. Donovan reminded himself that it was his father's work ethic that had eventually taken Donovan to college, leaving him without debt.

Nights like tonight made Donovan wonder at God's timing. He'd not been ready to attend church the first time Emily invited him. Tonight was perfect. The Bible-class lesson on Romans 13:8, "Let no debt remain outstanding, except the continuing debt to love one another, for he who loves his fellow man has fulfilled the law," meant so much more now that he'd seen exactly what loving his fellow man meant—especially fellow woman.

His feelings spread to his parents, to Jacob, Karl, Elise, Eva and even to Randall Tucker.

Leaving the building, he took Emily by the hand and entwined his fingers through hers. This was what home meant, not a building, not a town, but the right woman. He helped her into the truck, pleased when she grinned at him and scooted over to the middle. Hurrying around the vehicle, he thought about his next step. Ice cream tonight? A drive?

His phone sounded. He pulled it from his pocket and checked the name on the screen.

He had a message on his phone. Recognizing the number, he winced.

"Bad news?" Emily asked.

"It's my current boss, Nolan Tate. I haven't severed the relationship with him yet."

She managed to look sympathetic, but it made him consider. Did she even have a boss? She was in charge of the museum and it looked as though almost half the stuff had been donated by her family or, in the instance of the Majestic, purchased by her. The storytelling was something she did for fun. She didn't charge for it, not that he could see. The waitressing, she did in a pinch if her family needed her. And her boss was her father.

Donovan had some experience with fathers who were bosses.

First his own father and then Olivia's.

He swiped the on button and said, "Hello."

"Had an interesting call a few hours ago," Nolan said. "Have to say I'm surprised. This is something you should have discussed with me."

"It happened fast. He approached me Sunday and then again last night. I like it here. I think I'm ready to stay put. Did he offer to pay off my debt?"

There was that word again, from church.

"He did."

By the sound of Nolan's voice, Donovan couldn't tell if the offer had been satisfactory and taken or turned down.

If Nolan turned Tucker down, Donovan would have only five weeks.

Looking over at Emily, he figured five years, five decades, five lifetimes wouldn't be enough. He wanted forever.

"I told him I'd think about it."

Donovan let out a breath. He was so ready that he almost offered to pay Nolan more if the offer from Tucker wasn't satisfactory.

Not good.

He and Nolan never had what Donovan considered a close relationship. Nolan believed bigger was better. His whole life personified that belief. His voice boomed. He stood over six feet. And wherever he went, he expected to be first in line.

Donovan was ashamed to admit he'd started

appreciating the lifestyle. He'd been embarrassed by it at first, but front-row seats at professional sports games, no waiting at restaurants and vacations where every whim was adhered to—now, that was something.

He'd liked being called sir. He'd liked having the most beautiful woman in the room on his arm. He'd fallen in love with that, he now recognized, not with her.

It was so different than what he'd grown up with. His parents gave to God first, paid the bills and purchased necessities next, and if there was anything left over, they saved it. He'd missed out on a lot of childhood fun, at least to his mind. When he turned twelve, he'd asked for wages.

What do you need wages for? His dad had honestly been surprised.

I want to play baseball next year.

It's too far. You know it's too far into town and affects—

I know that. I intend to buy a car. I can drive myself. I want to play baseball.

He'd wanted to play baseball since he was in third grade.

Baseball had been just one more dream pushed aside for the reality of living so far from town.

"I appreciate you considering it," Donovan said. "I know it might put you in a tough spot, but—"

"Olivia's getting married," Nolan said.

"Oh."

"Does that bother you?"

"Not in the least," Donovan answered honestly. He glanced over at Emily. She had her cell phone out and was scrolling through photos of little Naomi. The kid must have been the subject of a million texts by now. So far Donovan had seen Naomi sleeping. Naomi sleeping under a blanket. Naomi sleeping in her mother's arms. Naomi sleeping in her father's arms. Naomi and Jacob sleeping in a chair.

"It bothers me. I was hoping you'd get back together. You were good for her. Made her behave. Something I never seemed able to do."

Olivia had thrown her final tantrum, that Donovan witnessed, in a restaurant, complaining that the fish was cold. They brought her a new one. This time it was rubbery. Her father ate it, and the waitress brought Olivia something else. Donovan couldn't remember what it was, but the poor waitress, flustered, had spilled a few drops on the sleeve of Olivia's dress. The meal had been comped, the waitress in tears and the bad taste in Donovan's mouth wasn't from the food.

He'd broken the engagement the next day.

He'd met with Nolan and a lawyer two days after that. When he'd been handed the debt he owed to Nolan Tate, Donovan hadn't protested.

In truth, Nolan had been fair. When Nolan hired Donovan, he'd fronted him thousands of dollars to start over—all contingent on Donovan working for him, as both an architect and on-site builder. For the first year, it had been a profitable working arrangement for both.

Donovan had been slowly pulling himself out of debt and even paying back a few small businesses that had suffered after Brewster and Russell had gone bankrupt.

Then Olivia came home from Europe.

"I'm not the same man I was when I dated her, sir. I'm glad she's getting married. I hope she's happy."

"Me, too." Nolan harrumphed before ending the call.

Emily turned off her phone. "So, are you working for Tate Luxury Homes still?"

"Not sure."

So much had happened that Emily was ill prepared for the trustees meeting on Thursday. Between visitors, getting texts with photos from Eva documenting every moment of Naomi's journey home and putting together a five-year plan that was way past due, Emily was exhausted.

And she'd miss dinner tonight, meaning she might not see Donovan.

Tonight's meeting would have more to it than just a report on how she was marketing the Lost Dutchman Museum. A few years ago, she'd pushed for the trustees to purchase at least four acres from the Pearls. She'd expected and accepted the no. But now she had more to offer to motivate such a venture. Donovan didn't know it, but maybe building a Hopi living area would be the museum's biggest boon. It could be hands-on, right down to letting the children who came to the museum grind corn and paint pottery. She could take her storytelling to a new level with that type of backdrop.

Maybe another full-time employee would make it into the budget.

In five years.

That's how long Donovan would be here. And since he was living here, certainly he could finish Tinytown ahead of schedule. It didn't escape Emily's notice that she wasn't thinking beyond that magic number. So much had changed lately, especially her.

She hadn't been this excited over an idea since she'd graduated. Nervously, she straightened the front, restocking maps and pens. She even spent time in her office on the computer looking over the previous curator's plans.

It appeared just opening in the morning and closing at night was good enough for him.

A few times she went and stood by the door, staring at the grounds and admiring the Superstitions. She hated to imagine the replica Donovan would make of the Hopi multifamily structure as having air-conditioning, but this last day of June was already well past a hundred degrees and getting hotter by the minute.

One of her instructors in South Dakota had talked about the television show where modern families spent months living like the pioneers did. Emily didn't like the idea, but did wonder if maybe something on a lesser scale could be done. Students could live like the Hopi for a few days.

It would help when teaching about the past.

Emily shook her head.

Her dad always said her dreams were a world in themselves. And today she certainly felt inspired to dream.

A text came through from Donovan: Nolan Tate satisfied with offer from Tucker. I'll be here five years! Celebrate tonight?

After meeting, might be late, YES, she responded.

When the last visitor left, Emily cleaned off the table in her office, found the errant chairs for five and set a pitcher of water in the middle. She didn't like using red plastic cups, but it was all she had and she didn't want to run to the store.

Gregory Hamm was the first to arrive. He was Mike Hamm's single uncle, who'd retired and returned to Apache Creek a good decade ago, after being a lawyer in Tucson for years. Next was Thelma Tittle, a retired librarian who'd designed and run the library until two years ago. Then there was a husband and wife team, Trudy and Darryl

Feeney. They'd owned quite a few businesses in Apache Creek, including the Miner's Lamp, where Jane worked. He'd been a banker, she a teacher.

"Thanks for agreeing to meet with me," Emily said.

"We were about to call you," Darryl said. Everyone nodded, and suddenly Emily got the feeling that it wasn't she who was in charge of the meeting.

"I've made an agenda," she said.

Obediently, the trustees took it, read it over and said, "Let's hear your ideas."

She talked about the black-and-white Salado bowl and how it led to a request from a museum in New Mexico. She opened her laptop and showed them the traveling dinosaurs. She spoke about the library's festival last week and Donovan's idea to have a booth with real gold panning. "We could work with AJ's Outfitters so that two local businesses benefit," she said.

Then, she outlined Donovan's design for Tinytown and the offer he'd made to build a Hopi village, one that could be lived in.

They were impressed.

"Where will this village be?" Thelma asked.

"A few years ago, I brought up buying a few acres from the Pearls. I'm sure they'd give us a good price. After all—"

Darryl stopped her. "This is the one thing we wanted to talk to you about."

The other trustees nodded.

"We found out yesterday morning that the Pearls were made an offer Monday morning. It was accepted Wednesday."

"That was fast," Emily said weakly.

"Money talks."

Just like that, Emily knew who'd made the offer. Randall Tucker. And Donovan would be the builder.

He'd told her the truth, hadn't he?

It wouldn't be the Baer house or Karl's.

Chapter Seventeen

"Where's Emily?"

Cook was the only one around who might know the answer, and Donovan was starting to worry.

"Not sure. Could she be at Eva's? That's where everyone else is."

"I don't think so." Donovan walked out to the back porch. The restaurant was open, but without the Hubrecht clan, it felt empty. Even the guests were quieter than usual.

Donovan took out his phone and checked his texts. Nothing. He'd tried her a few times, both calling and texting. No reply. Well, it made good business sense not to be distracted by a phone during a meeting. Still, it was after six. Her meeting with the trustees started at four thirty. Maybe it was still going and he should just head over there.

To an empty parking lot.

He tried her phone again. No answer. He left the museum, driving down Main Street, looking at the Miner's Lamp, the convenience store and even the park.

Heading back to the Lost Dutchman Ranch, he pulled into Karl's place and looked around. Garrett had good hearing, because he came to the door and waved.

"I'm looking for Emily," Donovan said after rolling down the window.

"She's not here. I'd try Eva's."

Everyone except Emily was at Eva's, including Karl. Garrett even drove up as Donovan was leaving. No one seemed concerned.

"Maybe she went somewhere with the trustees," Jacob suggested. "Did you try the Miner's Lamp? Darryl and his wife own it."

"Drove by. Her truck's not there."

"Call me in an hour if you've not found her," Jacob said.

It took only a few minutes to get from Eva's to the ranch. Donovan spotted Emily's truck by the barn. Not where she usually parked. Donovan parked his truck next to hers, exited and went over to peer inside. The Lost Dutchman Ranch had five such vehicles, all similar. This was hers, all right. Inside were a small drill, a socket wrench, a dark blanket, a fire extinguisher, two flashlights and a clipboard.

A dozen pens and pencils were propped in a cup holder.

And crumpled on the passenger seat was a blueprint. His, the one he'd taken to her just the other day. It couldn't have been more mangled if she had thrown it on the ground and stomped on it.

Opening the door, he reached inside and pulled it toward him.

A jagged tear split one of Timmy's hand-drawn houses apart.

He ran his palm over the paper, smoothing it. Turning it over, he tried to fold it back into some semblance of straight. That's when he noticed the words and address penciled in the corner.

Pearl Ranch Parcel.

Pearl Road.

Once upon a time, he'd been a stickler for details. He'd not seen a need at the meeting with Tucker. Had Emily seen this and thought he'd sold her out?

He had to remind himself to breathe. It mattered that much.

Hurrying inside the barn, he skidded to a stop by Harold Mull, who was spraying something in Harry Potter's ear.

"Emily here?" Donovan asked.

"She took her horse and went out for a ride a good ten minutes ago. She looked mad enough to spit nails. What did you do to her?"

"Something incredibly stupid," Donovan protested. "I just need to talk to her. Where does she usually ride?"

To his surprise, Harold willingly supplied the

answer. "Straight up to the downed tree that acts like a bench. You'll notice another tree that leans thanks to a lightning strike. Go to the left of it and follow the trail all the way up."

"All the way up to what?"

"Her favorite spot. She calls the ride Ancient Trails Road."

Donovan now knew another reason she'd hated the Baer house. She'd probably named the road.

Harold didn't volunteer to saddle Cinderella, but he did fetch Donovan bottled water to take.

"My advice," Harold said as Donovan nudged Cinderella, "is grovel."

Lately, groveling seemed to be a way of life. Donovan had sort of groveled when trying to appease Nolan Tate after the breakup. Then, there'd been a bit of groveling when he'd tried to convince George Baer not to halt construction.

Problem was, Donovan wasn't sure exactly what he was groveling about today.

Because really, now that he had a soothing ten minutes behind him with a June wind going through his hair and a steady horse under him, he wasn't sure why Emily could be mad.

Because he hadn't told her?

Well, he'd not specifically asked where Tucker was thinking to build. Donovan had been happy it wasn't near the Baer place or Karl's.

And, really, if a neighborhood sprang up around

the museum, couldn't that mean not only more visitors to the museum, but also more volunteers?

He had every argument ready for when he found her. But the words died on his lips an hour later because, quite frankly, Emily Hubrecht, sitting cross-legged on a jagged rock that looked down across the Apache Creek landscape, was enough to stop his heart.

When had he fallen so in love with her?

Was it when she'd been gathering petitions?

Or when she'd crouched on her knees in front of a skeleton, just sure it was Native American?

Maybe it was the day she'd picked up old candy wrappers and beer cans because she was looking for clues to help her father.

Maybe it was at the hospital, in Karl's room, when she'd said a prayer, entwined her soft, warm fingers with his and got him to "Amen."

He'd felt the connection all the way to his heart.

Emily heard the horse and rose to her feet. Used to be, she visited this place two or three times a month. It had probably been six months since she'd found—made—time.

Donovan dismounted and led Cinderella over to where her horse was tethered. Then, he came to stand by her. "You mad at me?"

"More like disappointed."

"I found the blueprint in your truck."

"He's building a planned community at the base of the mountain."

"Used to be a ranch."

"Now it's wide-open land, with animals and vegetation and—"

"And owned by a family named Pearl who just sold it. It was bound to happen. What did you think? That somebody would buy it and just leave it as it was?"

"Maybe."

"I seem to remember your sister Elise teasing you that you needed to buy all the property by the Baer house."

Emily half smiled. "I'd like that."

"So," Donovan said, "what is it that made you so mad that you stood me up and rode all the way up here?" He grimaced. "I might not be able to walk for a week."

"It's me," she admitted. "I got all excited, thinking about the Hopi village you brought up. I started dreaming about what it could be and making plans. A few years ago, I wrote a proposal to the trustees and to the town of Apache Creek asking that they purchase a few acres next to the museum for expansion. We didn't have the funds. Still don't."

"You were thinking I'd need acres to build your village?"

"I was thinking big."

"I like the way you think."

He hesitantly joined her on the ledge of the rock, sitting down and carefully pulling her beside him.

Compromise had never been easy for her. So often, she just knew if things were left alone, it would be to the benefit of future generations.

But sometimes you had to let progress chart its path.

"I think," Donovan said, "that we can secure a couple of acres next to the museum. If Tucker won't donate them, I'll buy them."

"You'd do that for me?" It occurred to her that this was the second time in as many days that he'd handed her the possibility of a dream come true.

"I was planning on purchasing land. I'd already mentioned it to Tucker."

"You planning on retiring soon?"

"No." He laughed, and she thought he sounded younger, happier, in a way. "I'm going to try to convince my parents to come out here and retire."

"So then you'd need to be around for more than five years?"

He reached out a hand and cupped her check. She leaned into the roughness, felt a type of comfort, longing, she'd never experienced before.

"I've fallen in love with you," he admitted.

She closed her eyes, wishing she could trap this moment into an hour, into days or months, and just savor the exact time a dream came true.

This dream wasn't something he was offering

her. It wasn't something she could respond to with *You'd do that for me?* It was something that could only work if they offered it to each other. It was, *I'll do that for us.*

"I've fallen in love with you, too," she admitted, cupping his cheek and drawing him closer to her so that when he spoke, she could feel his warm breath against her lips.

"Then, I guess I'll be living here forever."

"Happily forever after," she agreed.

Behind them, Cinderella neighed her approval.

* * * * *

Don't miss these other
THE RANCHER'S DAUGHTERS
stories from Pamela Tracy:
Sisters find hope, love and redemption
in the Arizona desert.

FINALLY A HERO
SECOND CHANCE CHRISTMAS

Dear Reader,

I hope you enjoyed Emily and Donovan's story. I've long wanted to write it. Emily, the third "Rancher's Daughter," had to wait for her turn a long, long time.

I was blessed with a wonderful mother, but as an adoptee, I always wondered about the woman who wasn't around to raise me. What was she like? Who were her people? What history was I missing? Emily is always questioning, questing and creating worlds—anything to feel a connection to the mother she didn't have a chance to know. She can do that because she has the support of family and a firm foundation with God.

One thing she does well is appreciate what God's given her.

Donovan is a little rougher. He's the only child. It's never easy being the only one. Emily never experienced such a situation. It's hard for her to understand how he could walk away from his heritage. At the beginning of *Arizona Homecoming*, Donovan didn't have a clue what he had turned his back on, what he was missing. After a month of Hubrecht family dynamics, especially the company of Emily, he's rethinking the allure of having roots. He's missing the counsel of his father, the touch of his mother's hand. Best of all, he's turning back to God.

When he meets Emily, one thing he does well

is start to question, quest and create a future that includes both Emily and God.

A true happily-ever-after.

I love hearing from my readers. You can contact me at www.pamelatracy.com or visit the Craftie Ladies of Romance, www.craftieladiesofromance. blogspot.com, where quite a few Love Inspired authors have a community. Have a blessed day!

Pamela Tracy

LARGER-PRINT BOOKS!

GET 2 FREE
LARGER-PRINT NOVELS
PLUS 2 FREE
MYSTERY GIFTS

Love Inspired®
SUSPENSE
RIVETING INSPIRATIONAL ROMANCE

Larger-print novels are now available...

YES! Please send me 2 FREE LARGER-PRINT Love Inspired® Suspense novels and my 2 FREE mystery gifts (gifts are worth about $10). After receiving them, if I don't wish to receive any more books, I can return the shipping statement marked "cancel." If I don't cancel, I will receive 4 brand-new novels every month and be billed just $5.49 per book in the U.S. or $5.99 per book in Canada. That's a savings of at least 19% off the cover price. It's quite a bargain! Shipping and handling is just 50¢ per book in the U.S. and 75¢ per book in Canada.* I understand that accepting the 2 free books and gifts places me under no obligation to buy anything. I can always return a shipment and cancel at any time. Even if I never buy another book, the two free books and gifts are mine to keep forever.

110/310 IDN GH6P

Name	(PLEASE PRINT)	
Address		Apt. #
City	State/Prov.	Zip/Postal Code
Signature (if under 18, a parent or guardian must sign)		

Mail to the **Reader Service:**
IN U.S.A.: P.O. Box 1867, Buffalo, NY 14240-1867
IN CANADA: P.O. Box 609, Fort Erie, Ontario L2A 5X3

**Are you a current subscriber to Love Inspired® Suspense books
and want to receive the larger-print edition?
Call 1-800-873-8635 or visit www.ReaderService.com.**

* Terms and prices subject to change without notice. Prices do not include applicable taxes. Sales tax applicable in N.Y. Canadian residents will be charged applicable taxes. Offer not valid in Quebec. This offer is limited to one order per household. Not valid for current subscribers to Love Inspired Suspense larger-print books. All orders subject to credit approval. Credit or debit balances in a customer's account(s) may be offset by any other outstanding balance owed by or to the customer. Please allow 4 to 6 weeks for delivery. Offer available while quantities last.

Your Privacy—The Reader Service is committed to protecting your privacy. Our Privacy Policy is available online at www.ReaderService.com or upon request from the Reader Service.

We make a portion of our mailing list available to reputable third parties that offer products we believe may interest you. If you prefer that we not exchange your name with third parties, or if you wish to clarify or modify your communication preferences, please visit us at www.ReaderService.com/consumerschoice or write to us at Reader Service Preference Service, P.O. Box 9062, Buffalo, NY 14240-9062. Include your complete name and address.

LISLP15

REQUEST YOUR FREE BOOKS!
2 FREE WHOLESOME ROMANCE NOVELS
IN LARGER PRINT
PLUS 2
FREE
MYSTERY GIFTS

✿✿✿✿✿✿✿✿✿✿✿✿✿✿✿✿✿✿✿✿✿✿✿

HEARTWARMING™
✿✿✿✿✿✿✿✿✿✿✿✿✿✿✿✿✿✿✿✿✿✿✿

Wholesome, tender romances

YES! Please send me 2 FREE Harlequin® Heartwarming Larger-Print novels and my 2 FREE mystery gifts (gifts worth about $10). After receiving them, if I don't wish to receive any more books, I can return the shipping statement marked "cancel." If I don't cancel, I will receive 4 brand-new larger-print novels every month and be billed just $5.24 per book in the U.S. or $5.99 per book in Canada. That's a savings of at least 19% off the cover price. It's quite a bargain! Shipping and handling is just 50¢ per book in the U.S. and 75¢ per book in Canada.* I understand that accepting the 2 free books and gifts places me under no obligation to buy anything. I can always return a shipment and cancel at any time. Even if I never buy another book, the two free books and gifts are mine to keep forever.

161/361 IDN GHX2

Name _____ (PLEASE PRINT) _____

Address _____ Apt. # _____

City _____ State/Prov. _____ Zip/Postal Code _____

Signature (if under 18, a parent or guardian must sign) _____

Mail to the **Reader Service:**
IN U.S.A.: P.O. Box 1867, Buffalo, NY 14240-1867
IN CANADA: P.O. Box 609, Fort Erie, Ontario L2A 5X3

* Terms and prices subject to change without notice. Prices do not include applicable taxes. Sales tax applicable in N.Y. Canadian residents will be charged applicable taxes. Offer not valid in Quebec. This offer is limited to one order per household. Not valid for current subscribers to Harlequin Heartwarming larger-print books. All orders subject to credit approval. Credit or debit balances in a customer's account(s) may be offset by any other outstanding balance owed by or to the customer. Please allow 4 to 6 weeks for delivery. Offer available while quantities last.

Your Privacy—The Reader Service is committed to protecting your privacy. Our Privacy Policy is available online at www.ReaderService.com or upon request from the Reader Service.

We make a portion of our mailing list available to reputable third parties that offer products we believe may interest you. If you prefer that we not exchange your name with third parties, or if you wish to clarify or modify your communication preferences, please visit us at www.ReaderService.com/consumerschoice or write to us at Reader Service Preference Service, P.O. Box 9062, Buffalo, NY 14240-9062. Include your complete name and address.

HWI5

WESTERN WP PROMISES

YES! Please send me **The Western Promises Collection** in Larger Print. This collection begins with 3 FREE books and 2 FREE gifts (gifts valued at approx. $14.00 retail) in the first shipment, along with the other first 4 books from the collection! If I do not cancel, I will receive 8 monthly shipments until I have the entire 51-book Western Promises collection. I will receive 2 or 3 FREE books in each shipment and I will pay just $4.99 US/ $5.89 CDN for each of the other four books in each shipment, plus $2.99 for shipping and handling per shipment. *If I decide to keep the entire collection, I'll have paid for only 32 books, because 19 books are FREE! I understand that accepting the 3 free books and gifts places me under no obligation to buy anything. I can always return a shipment and cancel at any time. My free books and gifts are mine to keep no matter what I decide.

272 HCN 3070 472 HCN 3070

Name	(PLEASE PRINT)	
Address		Apt. #
City	State/Prov.	Zip/Postal Code

Signature (if under 18, a parent or guardian must sign)

Mail to the **Reader Service:**
IN U.S.A.: P.O. Box 1867, Buffalo, NY 14240-1867
IN CANADA: P.O. Box 609, Fort Erie, Ontario L2A 5X3

* Terms and prices subject to change without notice. Prices do not include applicable taxes. Sales tax applicable in N.Y. Canadian residents will be charged applicable taxes. This offer is limited to one order per household. All orders subject to approval. Credit or debit balances in a customer's account(s) may be offset by any other outstanding balance owed by or to the customer. Please allow 4 to 6 weeks for delivery. Offer available while quantities last. Offer not available to Quebec residents.

WPBPA16R